PADDY ON THE ISLAND

The island was floating on a jade green ocean. There were rocks, there were little sandy bays along the shore, but the whole place felt so remote he could not imagine it having any connection at all with the estate office, or Mr Jonathan Pickering, or the long, dull pavements of his home town.

And nothing, *nothing* hinted of any way of going back. His contract said a year, and that, so far as he could see, was what it was likely to be.

Also available in Beaver
by Ursula Moray Williams

Bogwoppit
Spid

PADDY ON THE ISLAND

Ursula Moray Williams

Illustrated by Tor Morisse

BEAVER BOOKS

A Beaver Book

Published by Arrow Books Limited
62-65 Chandos Place, London WC2N 4NW

An imprint of Century Hutchinson Ltd

London Melbourne Sydney Auckland
Johannesburg and agencies throughout
the world

First published in 1987 by Andersen Press
Beaver edition 1989

Made and printed in Great Britain
by Anchor Press Ltd
Tiptree, Essex

ISBN 0 09 959250 9

Contents

For my sons,
Andrew, Hugh, Robin & James
and all my family

1
Renting the Island

Paddy was buying an island.

He had money (a few pounds), he had plans, he had great determination. He was nine years old and clever. Very clever. He was always top of his class. It made school very boring.

But he would never have dreamed of buying anything so dramatic as an island if his family had not become so impossible to live with—his parents so unkind, his aunts so bossy and his friends for the most part so unattractive.

'I should like to leave them for ever!' Paddy told Judy as they strolled by the sea. 'Or if not quite for ever, then at least for a year. A whole year too, I mean! No letters, no phone calls, no come-back-and-see-Uncle-Freddie. Everything on my own terms. My private island.'

'Well, there's one for sale in the estate agent's,' said Judy, who was sometimes his friend. 'I saw it in the window this morning.'

Paddy left her at lightning speed. She caught up with him while he was reading the advertisement through the fly-spotted window-pane:

'ISLAND TO RENT ON ONE YEAR'S LEASEHOLD. SUITABLE TENANT ESSENTIAL. ENQUIRE WITHIN.'

Paddy was within in seconds. He shook off Judy on the doorstep.

'I'll tell you about it later,' he announced, and Judy had to go.

'Ah!' said the estate agent. 'I have the owner with me now. Would you care to step this way?'

The agent showed him into an odd little side room

where, in a very large brown chair, sat a very small brown man.

'Excuse me,' said the agent, 'I have several more people to see. Call me if you need me!'

He shut the door on Paddy and the owner of the island.

'Jonathan Pickering,' said the owner, holding out his hand without rising.

'Paddy Robbins,' said Paddy, and sat down.

'You are the fifth person I have seen since the advertisement went into the window,' said Jonathan Pickering, 'but they all turned it down. They think there is something wrong with my island. What makes you think *you* want it?'

Paddy explained. He was clear, he was forthright, honest and precise. His family had become impossible, he explained, and he wanted to go and live by himself on an island for a while, to be rid of them.

'What about education?' asked Jonathan Pickering shrewdly.

'I am well ahead of my schoolmates,' said Paddy coldly. 'I can well afford to miss a year's schoolwork and catch up later. Where is the island?'

'Well,' said the owner, 'that's not the point—not just yet. Don't you want to hear the terms of the leasehold?'

'Do you mean the rent?' Paddy asked.

'Not quite,' said Jonathan Pickering, 'there's more to it than that. I'm *letting* it, you see, not selling it. There are certain conditions . . . .'

'Why are you letting it?' Paddy interrupted, curious to know. (Perhaps the real owner was going abroad?)

'That's my business!' said Jonathan Pickering quite sharply. 'One of the conditions is that nobody renting it need expect any communication with the rest of the world while they are there, because if they do they aren't likely to get it.'

'Oh?' said Paddy, interested. This sounded to him more like an attraction than a drawback.

'No post. No telephone. No radio. No television!' said Jonathan Pickering. 'No link with civilisation for a whole year. Get it?'

Paddy nodded.

'What happens if you are ill?' he asked suddenly. His mother would have asked that first.

'You eat berries,' said Jonathan Pickering. 'Some of them will make you worse, and some will make you better. You have to try them to find out. But after all, the living's free!'

Paddy stared, nonplussed.

'What do you live on—to *eat*?' he asked uncertainly.

'Berries,' said Jonathan Pickering. 'And you catch fish and drink stream water. It is very cold and very good.'

'Is there a house on the island?' asked Paddy.

'There is quite a good hut. It has a squash court,' said Jonathan Pickering unexpectedly. 'You would have to take a racquet and ball. There are fishing rods too, and lines and hooks and things.'

'What do you use for bait?' asked Paddy.

'Berries,' said the owner. 'Some of them the fish like, and some of them the fish don't.'

'Is there a boat?' asked Paddy hopefully.

'No boat! I told you there were no communications,' said the owner. 'You fish off the rocks.'

'Is it a very big island?' Paddy suggested.

'Oh no, no! Not at all!' said Jonathan Pickering. 'Quite small. You could put it inside Regent's Park. It's a nice island,' he added. 'It's a very nice island indeed!'

'Aren't you—er—sorry to leave it?' suggested Paddy.

'Well yes, in a way! But I want a year off,' said Jonathan Pickering. 'I hope to travel. But first I must be sure of getting a reliable tenant. You see, I have one rather special object that I couldn't leave alone there to look after itself....'

Paddy listened, alert, but he was disappointed.

'I don't think I need tell you what it is,' pursued the owner. 'It won't make much difference to you, not knowing. But it will make a tremendous difference to *me* if I know it isn't left there all alone without a guardian. Someone could go in and steal it...' he mused.

'I wouldn't let them!' Paddy cried, fired with enthusiasm.

'Quite, quite!' said Jonathan Pickering, coolly. 'But you aren't very old, are you? Are your parents going with you, by the way? No, I think you told me not.'

'Not on your life!' said Paddy hotly. 'Nobody is going with me!'

'That's just as well,' said Jonathan Pickering, 'because another condition of the lease is that there shall never be more than two people on the island at one time.'

'Two?' asked Paddy, surprised.

'Yes, two. You see, what seems like a little paradise to you at this moment may become quite a nightmare when you have been there for a week or so. You'd do better to make up your mind early who you really want to live with, and stick to it.'

'But I don't want to live with anybody!' Paddy cried. 'Besides, if one can't telephone or write letters or send a cable, how is one going to let anybody know that one needs them?'

'Ah!' said Jonathan Pickering wisely, closing one eye in a wink. 'That's what all the other people said! They thought there was something fishy about the whole affair. Never mind! A tenant is bound to turn up in time. Don't worry about it, dear boy, don't worry!'

The door opened and the estate agent poked his face into

the room.

'There's another couple come about the island, Mr Pickering,' he announced. 'Have you finished with this young man? Shall I show them in?'

'No, no! No! I want it! I really want it!' Paddy cried, bouncing about on his chair. 'I'd like to take it, please Mr Pickering, for a year. I mean it! How much is the rent?'

Jonathan Pickering shrugged his shoulders.

'We can talk about that at the end of the year,' he said, 'but it won't be very much, in any case. You have made up your mind, then? Are you sure? Do you really want to rent my island? Or do you mean you would like to think it over during the night?'

'But the new people may want it at once!' Paddy protested. 'No, please! I'd like to take it now. Where is it?' he asked as an afterthought.

'You had better sign this paper,' said Jonathan Pickering.

The estate agent brought a paper, on which Paddy Robbins was designated as the tenant of an island belonging to J. Pickering Esq. He agreed, the paper said, to rent the island for a year. His tenancy would begin on the following morning. That would give him time, the owner explained, to collect a squash racquet, some tins of food, and any other objects he wished to take with him.

'Books?' added Jonathan Pickering. 'Do you read?'

'Quite a lot,' Paddy admitted, 'but things seem to come into my head without it.'

'Hmm!' said Jonathan Pickering, signing his name under Paddy's. 'You're lucky! Well, I hope you will enjoy your tenancy while you are there.'

'But where *is* it?' asked Paddy.

'Come back in the morning and I'll tell you,' said Jonathan Pickering, with another wink.

The estate agent was already taking the advertisement out of the window.

2
Paddy at Home

Judy was loitering on the corner of the street but Paddy passed her by with a vague dismissal of the hand, and she fell way, disappointed.

He ought, Paddy was thinking, to ask just one or two more questions about the tenancy. If Jonathan Pickering would not tell him, then the agent might. He turned in his tracks, brushed past Judy for the second time, and climbed the steps of the estate office.

The door was locked. A blind had come down over the windows and there was no movement inside. Within five short minutes the place had ceased to function. He was so upset he felt like kicking in the door.

'Did you see them come out?' he demanded of Judy.

'No. Nobody came,' she said, glad to be of any help at all.

'Then there must be a door at the back,' said Paddy, but although he turned the corner into the next street he could see no entrance that could possibly lead into the estate agent's office from the back, only rows and rows of dull little houses.

Paddy made one more effort to be heard. He rang the bell and knocked loudly on the closed door, all under the eyes of Judy, who could not bear to go away. He felt humiliated by her watching, and by the hopelessness of having no attention paid to him at all—he, who had just become the temporary owner of an island.

'Why do you want them so badly?' Judy asked.

'I am renting an island for a year,' said Paddy proudly, 'and I want to ask for a few more details. I wish you would go away, Judy! I shan't have any time to be with you now. I'll see you in—in about a year's time . . . .'

'Oh!' she said, shocked, then defiantly: 'Why on earth didn't you ask them the details before? If I'd been with you I'd have asked them a thousand things! It would be silly not to! You weren't in there very long . . . .'

'Look here,' said Paddy with icy calm, 'will you just—get out?'

'All right,' she said humbly, and then with a ray of hope: 'Where is the island, Paddy? Will you write?'

'No,' he said decidedly, 'and I don't know where the island is. That's what I'm trying to find out.'

Judy's mouth came open and remained agape. She closed it at last to stammer: 'When are you going?'

'In the morning,' said Paddy shortly. He ran past her this time and did not stop until he reached home. Once, still running, he half turned to wave her goodbye, but Judy too was running, in the opposite direction.

Paddy was tormented all night long by the thought of the island he had agreed to rent for a year. He did not even know how to get there. Judy, however annoying and persistent, would at least have got some information about that, for Judy was a very practical girl, but she was the very last person he could ever imagine needing on an island of his own.

His parents were out. One aunt was gardening, and the other tormenting the strings of a violin upstairs. She could only do this when his parents were absent, and Paddy's complaints carried no weight with her, though he walked pointedly into the house with his hands covering his ears.

'Take off your shoes!' called the gardening aunt but he took no notice of her either.

He went up to his bedroom and opened all the drawers.

Presumably he would need a change of clothes, though not as many as his mother thought. And a model kit? He left this on the bed but packed a toothbrush. No need, even if he were marooned, to live like a savage. He added a comb.

What discouraged him most were the questions that his family were bound to ask him, and he could not make up his mind whether to tell them he was leaving or not.

What island? Where was the island? What about school? What about church-on-Sundays? What about food? What about illness? Berries! What kind of berries? Poisonous berries? How poisonous? Deadly berries? How would he be able to tell the difference? 'Some made you worse and some didn't!' But *which* didn't? 'Well, those were the ones that made you better!'

The gardening aunt came in to make the tea. He certainly was not going to tell *her* anything about it.

'Would you like some toast?' she asked him kindly.

'No thanks,' said Paddy, and then remembered that he might not taste toast again for a year. 'Yes please,' he added quickly.

Over his tea Paddy took a pencil and paper to write out a list of the companions he would *not* want to invite to the island. Actually he did not want any at all, but there was no harm in writing down the names of those who deserved to be totally neglected, and he began the list with: 'Aunts One and Two.'

'You'll get butter on the paper, dear,' said the gardening aunt, passing by with the teapot. 'Can't you do your homework later?'

Paddy ate his toast and continued to write his list.

The aunt took the teapot and a cup in to the violin aunt. There was a brief respite from the music.

'If *I* played the violin . . . ' Paddy thought, 'I would do it a great deal better than that!'

Idly, he wrote 'Judy' on his list, and followed it with the names of several more friends and relations. Then he wrote

'Judy' again, and underlined it. He did not write the names of his parents. It seemed too drastic. After all, they were his parents and could not help, he supposed, being so disagreeable. Not that he thought for a single minute of asking them to come and see him on the island.

'Clear your tea away, Paddy, and wash up the tea things!' called the gardening aunt, coming back into the room. She dumped two cups and saucers and two plates into the kitchen sink and went back into the garden.

The violin aunt came in to put her violin away.

'Have you ever been on an island, Aunt Jay?' Paddy asked.

'Yes, of course I have,' she said brightly, polishing her bow with a duster. 'I've been to the Isle of Wight and the Isle of Man, and Skye, Iona, Mallorca and Cyprus. They're all islands.'

'Yes, but I mean a little island,' Paddy said. 'One about the size of Regent's Park. Do you think it would be nice?'

'I shouldn't think so at all,' said the violin aunt. 'There wouldn't be much to do there, would there? No concert hall, no shops, no swimming pool, if the sea was cold or rough. And no entertainments. I shouldn't think there would be much of an hotel, either. Of course, if it were quite an empty island I might be able to practise my music without the fuss and commotion it makes when I do it here . . . ' she added wistfully.

Paddy made a face.

'I just wanted to know,' he said shortly.

What would happen, he asked himself, if after all he did *not* go to the island? True, he had signed a paper, but nobody could force him to go if he stuck in his heels and told the police about it. He was under age, after all.

For a moment home seemed warm and kindly, till he remembered the washing-up, and rose with a sigh to rattle the china in lukewarm water, while both aunts shouted at him to take great care not to chip the cups and saucers.

Much later his parents came in from work. The table was laid all over again.

'Have you done your homework?' they both asked him.

He had not.

If, tomorrow, he was going to be far away on an island of his own (for a year) there was no point in filling pages of exercise books with facts and figures of which he would not hear the result.

He and his father dived for the television at the same moment and cracked their heads together too hard for comfort.

'Well *really*!' exclaimed his mother fretfully.

While they were arguing the blame the gardening aunt came in and turned on a gardening programme. The musical aunt wanted a concert on Radio Three and a considerable discussion followed, during which Paddy took the bump on his forehead up to his bedroom and slammed the door.

'You might have told him you were sorry,' he heard his mother say as he left the room.

'Well who pays for the television licence I'd like to know!' said his father crossly. Gentle pictures of spring gardens drifted on to the screen.

Paddy decided *not* to tell his parents that he was leaving them for a year to live by himself on an island.

3
The First Day on the Island

'Can I borrow your squash racquet, Dad?' Paddy asked in the morning.

'All right. Put it back!' said his father, preoccupied with papers.

'Is there a ball?'

'Somewhere.'

His parents went off to work.

Till the last minute Paddy wanted to fling his arms round their necks and tell them he was going away, but they were in such a hurry . . . .

Neither of them offered to help him find the squash ball. He did stand on the steps to see them go but they never turned round to see him waving.

The aunts went upstairs to make beds.

Paddy found the squash ball, picked up the racquet and his weekend bag, and left the house as if he were on his way to school as usual.

This morning the estate office was open. Paddy walked up the steps not knowing quite what would happen next.

What he did not expect was to push open the door on to the golden sands of a tropical island, with hundreds of miles of ocean between him and the horizon whichever way he looked.

And it was so beautiful! Paddy never remembered being impressed by beauty before—not since the transformation scene at the Christmas pantomime. But there it had all been movement and glittering figures, while here it was utterly still and peaceful, save for the shimmering, dancing waves, the gently ululating palm leaves overhead and the scuffling of his own feet in the sand.

The sand was so yellow, and the blue sea so blue! Where the leaves were green they were intensely, vividly green, while the small white clouds in the sky fluttered past as white as the cabbage butterflies that annoyed the aunts in his mother's garden.

The island was floating on a jade green ocean. There were rocks, there were little sandy bays along the shore, but the whole place felt so remote he could not imagine it having any connection at all with the estate office, or Mr Jonathan Pickering, or the long, dull pavements of his home town.

And nothing, *nothing* hinted of any way of going back. His contract said a year, and that, so far as he could see, was what it was likely to be.

It was small, as the owner had said. Looking back he could see the sea glinting through the palm trees, while to the north and south lay wide, clean beaches with rocks and little pools, and the shadowy entrances to caves. That reminded him of Jonathan Pickering's 'treasure', and he determined to explore them one by one.

In the very middle of the island stood the house that Jonathan Pickering had talked about, and beside it a squash court, littered with twigs and little stones. The hut was quite pleasant. There was just the one room but each of the four windows looked out in a different direction and framed a beautiful view.

There was a bed, with blankets and a pillow, a table and a chair and a cooking stove. Plenty of matches, not even damp ones, and a battered saucepan for cooking whatever there was to cook. And there was a mouth organ on the shelf above the bed. Paddy used it to prevent the squash ball from falling on to the floor.

Then he went outside and leaned against a tree.

'This is my first day, and my first *hour* on my own island,'

Paddy thought, 'and I shall always want to remember just what I felt like at the very beginning.'

After a pause he began to walk the whole way round the island and it did not take him long. He left the caves till later and kept to the sands, keeping an eye open for wild life, like crocodiles or snakes or monkeys, but seeing nothing at all.

Birds sang but he could not see them, and there were berries of all shapes and sizes on the little bushes under the trees. Some of them looked delicious. He would have to try them very carefully to find out which were unwise to eat, and which were just nice—or very nice indeed.

Meanwhile he nibbled at a Mars bar in his pocket. Yes, he might save it of course, but what was the point? Once it was gone it was gone, and he would have to get used to living on just berries.

At some time he had kicked off his shoes and shed his jacket. He was walking with bare feet, in his shorts and shirt. It all felt utterly delicious. When the Mars bar smeared his shirt he shed that too, and now he was King of the Island in just his shorts, with breezes blowing gently over his bare chest, and no aunt within a thousand miles to tell him to go and brush his hair.

'Now I am going to forget time,' said Paddy, and he stopped on the sand to draw a circle with his toe.

'That's me, and that's now, and after that there is no more anything for a year!' Paddy murmured. 'No meal times, no bed time, no waking-up time. I shall eat when I'm hungry and go to bed when I feel sleepy. I shall live exactly as I please, now and for always. Amen!'

He felt so free he began to run and jump and turn cartwheels, shouting at the top of his voice. He leapt at the palm fronds and swung to and fro scuffing the sand with his bare toes as they swept across it. He dived into the sand and kicked it in all directions. He threw little stones into the sea and raced into the ripples to kick them back to the shore. He found a ribbon of seaweed, and ran about shouting and waving it like a flag. And all the time the island was smiling and dancing with him. This was joy for ever. This was Life.

Presently he was hungry, and wandered into the shrubs and bushes seeking food. How agreeable to pick your own dinner from the twigs and the branches and to crunch between your teeth the nutty delicious berries with ten times more flavour than a roasted peanut! And how good to nibble at leaves as brittle and tasty as potato crisps! After which he discovered a cool and bubbling spring, where he drank deeply, and thought it tasted better than Coca-Cola or lemonade.

Then he flung himself down under a shady tree and slept in the warm sunshine, with the breeze like a soft blanket tickling his chin.

When he awoke there was a golden tinge to the island light. If anyone was forced to recognise time it must be afternoon.

'I think I shall have a game of squash,' Paddy said, brushing the sand off his legs. He wandered back to the house.

He had never really learnt the game, but the court, though rough, was easy, and the ball came flying at him more times than he could hit it back. Presently he was quite exhausted.

Putting on his shirt he strolled down to the shore, mouth organ in hand, and sat on a rock, looking out to sea and dreaming quietly. He watched the velvet darkness creeping gently towards him across the water. Fireflies danced under the palm trees. Phosphorescence flickered over the waves. The moon rose like a flower out of the sea, and hung in the sky, much closer than the stars.

'I'm happy!' Paddy murmured. 'And I'm going to be happy for a whole year! Then maybe I'll persuade Jonathan Pickering to make another contract so I can be happy for ever and ever!'

4
Cat

In the morning he ate a feast of berries and played several games of squash.

Later in the day he intended to go fishing. If he caught any he would fry the fish and eat it, and use the bits he didn't want for bait. Meanwhile he had to fish with paper worms. Not a single bite came to any of his berries.

He was carrying home his catch—a large fat plaice, bigger than any he had seen in the freezer compartment of the supermarket, and of course bigger than the little ones they sold in the shops. It would have been gratifying to show it to Judy, and certainly his father.

But there was nobody to show it to, till he reached the steps of the house, on which was sitting, very composed and elegant, a large white cat. A very large, very fat white cat.

'Oh!' said Paddy, stopping short in surprise.

The cat opened its mouth and spat. Or it might have sneezed. They stood staring at one another.

Then the cat caught sight of the fish, and its whiskers quivered. It sprang forward, and all but snatched the plaice out of Paddy's hand, but he twitched it out of the way.

'Oh no you don't!' said Paddy angrily. 'That's my dinner! You can go and catch your own fish, my boy!'

'I am not your boy, and I am going to have kittens and I am very hungry,' returned the cat, thrashing its tail to and fro.

'Then what are you doing *here*?' Paddy asked in alarm. Jonathan Pickering had never mentioned anything about a cat. And if only two people at a time were allowed on the island, what kind of a difference would kittens make?

'Do you belong to Mr Pickering?' he added. Suddenly he wondered if this might not possibly be Jonathan Pickering's 'treasure'.

'Mister who? Never heard of him! No of course I don't!' said the cat. 'I came from the sea. And I don't know where I am. That brute of a second mate threw me into the water!'

'What?' said Paddy, shocked. 'Just like that?'

'Just like that!' said the cat. It turned its head towards the sea and spat several times quite spitefully. 'If I hadn't found a piece of driftwood to cling to we'd all have been drowned,' it added sadly.

'Will you tell me—are you what one might call a—a person?' Paddy asked, a little embarrassed.

'Yes of course I am. Aren't you?' said the cat. 'Why do you want to know?'

'Well as it happens I'm renting this island from Mr Jonathan Pickering,' Paddy explained with a certain importance. 'In fact, it is my private island for a whole year. And in my contract it says that no more than two people may be on the island at the same time. Do you know how many kittens you may be likely to have?'

'No I don't,' said the cat. 'I didn't know I was going to have any kittens at all till the sailors told me, and then the second mate threw me overboard. Can you imagine anything so heartless? Do get on and cook that fish. I'm so hungry I could cry! I mean, please do cook it, and give me a share!'

Paddy went into the hut and the white cat followed. Apart from the worry about the kittens it was rather a nice cat, Paddy thought. It was independent and intelligent and quite good company. Not that he needed company, Paddy told himself hastily, but suppose one did, a cat like this would fit the bill.

'Do stay as long as you like,' he invited, adding quickly:

'I mean, until your kittens are born!'

'Well I don't know where I'm to go after that,' said the cat plaintively. It sat anxiously watching the fish being grilled, and twitched its whiskers to the appetising smell of the toasting flesh.

'Which end do you want?' the cat asked when the cooking was three parts done. 'Because I prefer the head end if it's all the same to you....'

Paddy was handing the fish to the cat on the end of a stick when the door of the hut opened and a boy looked in.

'Yummy!' said the boy.

He was the same size as Paddy, and might have been older or might have been younger. His hair was a deep, rich red, and his eyes were very dark brown. He wore beach shoes, old jeans and a cotton tee-shirt, with ITS ME written across it in blue letters.

He grinned at Paddy and held out his arms to the cat, who leapt into them, dragging the fish by the backbone.

'I thought you would be here when I smelled the fish,' the boy said to the cat, hugging it.

Paddy went cold with dismay. Now there were *three* on the island, and the contract was already broken. But nothing awful was happening yet. On the other hand all of a sudden his privacy was completely shattered. And so soon too! How could Jonathan Pickering have cheated him like that?

'It's all right, I'm not staying,' the boy said, as if reading his thoughts. 'I only came after my cat! It belongs to my grandpa who is captain of the *Princess Daisy*, and one of the stupid sailors threw it into the sea. Somebody saw it floating away on a piece of wood, so I pinched the little dinghy and rowed after it. I shan't half catch it from my grandpa, but the mate caught it even worse! He's on bread-and-water till we get home! Serves him right, don't you think? He thought it brought bad luck to have cats on board, let alone kittens! What are you doing here anyway? Having a holiday? Where are your folks? There's nowhere much for them to be on a place like this!'

Paddy explained.

'Do you mean it?' the boy exclaimed. 'All by yourself? For a whole year? Your very own island? You are lucky! I thought I had all the luck going on a voyage with my grandpa, but I'd rather have an island of my own!'

'The only thing is . . . ' Paddy said, 'I was warned that there must never be more than two people on the island together, and now we are three, and there may be lots more quite quickly. . . .'

'Don't be daft! Blossom's only a cat!' said the boy, hugging the white cat, fishbones and all. It kicked and struggled and choked in an effort to assert itself, and then dangled from his arm, chewing bones. 'Don't take any notice of what she tells you! Yes, I'd love a bit of fish, but only a little bit. There's quite a good dinner waiting for me, I guess, on board and I don't want them setting sail without me! Thanks, that's plenty! Keep the rest of it for yourself! I'll be off before the weather changes. I hope you enjoy your stay. I don't expect you will have many visitors after me. It's such miles away from anywhere!'

'Can't you stay, just a couple of hours?' Paddy said, for the boy was just the sort he would like all his friends to be.

'Sorry,' said the boy. 'They don't know I'm gone, you see. Give me another bit of fish for Blossom, and we'll be off. There will be ever such a scene when they can't find me, and when they find the boat is gone too. I guess there will be hell to pay! Do you want to come with me and see the fun? No, I thought you wouldn't! All right then, I'll leave you. Happy days! 'Bye, I'm off!'

He was gone before Paddy remembered to ask him his name or where the island was.

It was all rather unsettling. First the white cat and then the visiting boy. Paddy watched the little boat row steadily away towards the horizon, and presently it passed beyond it and was lost.

He wished it had never come. Everything had been going fine before that happened. And the mere sight of the boy rowing the boat so steadily with the white cat sitting in the bows made him realise how useful a little boat could be. It was really the one thing that the island lacked.

He walked down to the shore and looked far out to sea. The boat had disappeared. A slight dullness on the edge of the horizon spoke of coming night.

It had been so nice before they came, Paddy grumbled to himself. Everything had been just about perfect. And it still was, of course. He was glad they hadn't stayed, but he wasn't glad they had come—at least it felt something like that. It was just, well unsettling, and the island didn't feel quite so much his own any longer.

But it was his own!

Only, he couldn't help feeling—if the boy's grandpa was mad at the boy going off for an hour or two, what were his own parents going to be at *his* going off for a whole year? It really was a bit unkind that he had not left a message or said goodbye to them. He didn't mind so much about the aunts. Yet the musical one had given him a Mars bar . . . .

Thoughtfully he dug a hole in the sand and buried the fishbones that the cat hadn't eaten.

5
In the Cave

'You need expect no communication with the outside world!' Jonathan Pickering had said, but already the world had crashed in upon him. First the cat, and then the boy, and far off beyond the horizon their ship, the *Princess Daisy*. If it had happened once it might happen again.

Paddy was deeply disturbed. Half of him wanted the island as it had been when he arrived and for a little while afterwards, and half of him thought with wistful envy of the fluffy white cat and the lively, friendly boy, either of which might have made ideal companions.

He found himself eyeing the horizon in search of a sail or a funnel, or some signs of a boat, large or small. He even looked for smoke trails in the sky, as if some invisible aircraft might be spying on him—looking out for a place to land.

Nothing arrived by land or by sea or by air. But he wouldn't have even *thought* of them, Paddy told himself, if it had not been for the cat or the coming of the boy.

Just supposing the cat had stayed, all by itself, and its master the boy had not found it? If it was so easy to track down a cat sitting on a piece of driftwood anyone else might find the island and come too—maybe a whole ship full of people.

This idea put Paddy into such a bad mood that for a whole day he sat brooding on the rocks, looking out to sea and cursing the trespassers, both those who had trespassed and those who seemed likely to do so. Even the cat, who had eaten by far the greater part of the fish. Tiresome, greedy, maddening animal. For the first time Paddy felt some sympathy towards the second mate.

Already he had lost count of the days he had been on the island. That was fine. That was as it should be, but there was a drawback. If he became too used to living without time (his watch had stopped long ago) wasn't it going to be a fearful shock when the year came to an end, and he thought he was only halfway through his tenancy? He decided to drop a stone into the tin mug belonging to the hut first thing every morning when he came out into the sunshine. It meant he never brushed his teeth, but the berries didn't seem to make them very dirty.

He found he missed conversation. There was nothing and nobody to talk to. No animals, very few birds, absolutely nothing comparable with a monkey or a dog or a cat. The mouth organ was good company and he also played a solo kind of squash until the ball burst, and there was nothing to hit except shreds of rubber. Then he played with fircones or similar, which would not bounce, or berries, which burst, and the more expert he became at the game the quicker the balls seemed to wear out.

He had, of course, explored the caves in search of Jonathan Pickering's 'treasure'. But there was nothing to be found, and nowhere at all to hide anything of value. He had even tried to move the rocks, but nothing even trembled.

There was so much time to do anything in. Paddy would not admit he could ever feel the least bit discontented, yet here he was, scowling at the sun, kicking at the rocks, staring at the sea, longing for something to appear that he could shout 'GO AWAY' to.

Instead, he found a small board and wrote on it in pencil: 'PRIVATE. DO NOT LAND.' He propped this against a rock, facing out to sea, and then secretly hoped no one would see it and pass by before he had time to inspect them. The boy? The cat?

No. No boy. No cat.

He kicked a pebble the whole way round the island, and ate a great many leaves and berries until they tasted of nothing any more.

He fished and caught more fish than he could eat, so threw them back again. He slept in the sun. When he woke, it was nearly dark. He swam a little.

His tin was rattling with morning pebbles when he secretly suspected that doing nothing was only one degree worse than being bossed by aunts.

He missed his parents.

He missed his school friends.

He missed Judy.

He missed his class work.

He almost missed his aunts.

He missed things like Mars bars, ice cream, potato crisps, salt, sweets, getting ahead of the rest of the class, having something to read, finding out problems, chicken to eat, bread sauce, binoculars, photographs, a ruler, computers, cool drinks, television, television, television—yes he did, he did, he did . . . .

But he would not admit it.

If the cat had not come, Paddy thought, it would all have been perfect. And he slammed a stone into the base of a tree.

The cat was bad enought, but the boy was worse. He and the boy could have competed, quarrelled, argued, disputed, and exchanged long stories. They could have made things together and played football, cricket, and played 'Desert Island Discs' on the mouth organ.

They could have invented terrible punishments for the bossy aunts. And then they could have forgiven them and invited them to a fabulous supper party of fish and berries and leaves. But the mere thought of aunts on the island was impossible, and his skin crept.

Why, Paddy thought, as the days went by, was he only thinking dreadful thoughts? Why not cheer himself up with nice ones? Or why think anything at all? Why have to think? Why not just *be*?

Paddy wandered into the caves for the twentieth time and saw a crack in one corner that he had not noticed before.

It wasn't *there* before! Paddy thought indignantly, as he walked across to inspect it.

It ran from ceiling to floor, and was just wide enough for a boy to slip inside. Paddy slipped.

He did not stop to wonder whether the rocks were moving. Or whether, once inside, he could ever get out again.

It looked like a perfectly straightforward crack—a narrow passage running into the hill above the cave. It looked as if it had been there for ever. Paddy thought it had not, but at least it looked as if it had come to stay. When he put his hand on the walls they were as solid as eternity. When he pushed at the sides with his shoulders the whole weight of the hill pushed back and nothing moved at all.

He did not hesitate but slid into the crack and followed it far, far into the back of the cave, and beyond the cave into the hill.

Yes it was dark! But high about him some far daylight seeped down into the passage and led him on. It never grew any darker, but neither was there any more light. His eyes grew used to the twilight, and his feet to the cool damp of the sand he walked on.

As he walked his spirits rose. Here at last was something new to do! He had become used to the island. It was so small there was nothing left to explore, but this *was* exploring, and from one corner to the next he did not know what to expect. Perhaps the passage went all the way through the hill and came out on the shore on the far side, like a thread? He didn't remember any caves there, but the passage could burrow out of the grass like a rabbit hole.

However, it did not. After a long, long walk it ended quite abruptly in a round cave that seemed to announce quite plainly: This passage ends here. It goes no further. Paddy was disappointed. It all seemed to have come to nothing at all.

The cave was empty, except for one large flat stone lying in the middle of it. Paddy kicked the stone with his foot and it moved. He knelt down to pick it up and the stone came agreeably to his hand. Underneath it was another stone, just as large and smooth and flat as the first. Paddy put his fingers to the edge of the second stone and scraped away the sand that surrounded it.

The second stone too moved quite easily. Underneath it was a third stone, much wider and heavier, and even flatter—more like the opening to a tomb. Paddy pushed away the sand and dug at the stone. It moved a little and he dug again.

After a while he was able to tip it on one side and drag it out of the hole he had made. Now there were three stones lying beside him on the floor of the cave, also a considerable heap of sand where he had scrabbled around them. And underneath the third stone there was a slab.The slab was made of rock. It was broad and long, and looked like the lid of a box.

Paddy's heart began to beat. Right from the beginning of the crack he had had the premonition that this might be the clue to Jonathan Pickering's treasure, and with the lifting of each stone he became more and more sure that he was right.

A crack, where there had appeared to be no crack before.

A long winding walk through narrow rocks in the half dark. A round, vaulted empty cavern, and a stone—one stone, a second stone, a third stone, and now the unmistakable lid of a stone chest. It had to be Jonathan Pickering's treasure.

Now that he was sure, Paddy stopped short. He wondered if he ought to go any further. The treasure was buried. It had every appearance of being secret and hidden. He had promised to look after it, to defend and protect it. He had not been told what it was, nor given permission to find out.

The stone lid was sunk so far into the sand that he doubted if he could move it if he tried, but a fearful curiosity made him walk round and round it like a cat, and kneel beside it to dig his fingers under the edges and feel it to see if there were any way of lifting it up at all.

He began to scoop handfuls of sand away from the sides until the lid stood proud of its bed, and once free he could not bear to bury it again.

He scooped away more sand, till the lid was exposed on a little plateau, but there was no way of telling if it covered a box or a chest, or was so large that it went down deep, deep into its bed beneath the floor of the cave. There seemed to be no way at all of opening it. No lock. No handle.

Sure by now that he was doing wrong in persisting, Paddy gave the slab a violent shove, and to his great surprise it slid easily across the sandy floor in front of him, tucking itself into the soft pile of sand as if it belonged there.

After all, there was no box, no safe, no locked treasure chest. There was just a flight of steps leading down into the darkness . . . .

6
?

Now Paddy was frightened.

He had become used to the twilight and the remoteness of the passage and the lonely cavern. He had plucked up his courage to move the stones but he had never expected to find a final problem like this one.

It was too much and he tried frantically to put things back as they had been when he found them. But the more he pulled and struggled the more obstinately the slab sank down into the sand, and the more sand went pouring down the dark stairs into the unknown depths below.

Something, Paddy felt, was down there waiting for him. He didn't know what, but it was something . . . .

When all his efforts failed, when nothing would budge the stone a single inch—the stone that had slid so easily out of place—Paddy turned and fled.

Who knew what would or could come up those long, dark steps? There was a fearful sensation of everlasting nothingness that at any moment would change into a horrible shape moving towards him. Above all, Paddy longed for a door to slam between him and It, but there was nothing. The three flat stones sat smugly side by side above the hole. The last large flat rock lay solidly apart. Immovable, indifferent.

A small black cloud of emptiness seemed to hover above the hole. But Paddy was gone. Panting, gasping, he thrust his way back along the passage, which seemed narrower and longer than ever. He grazed his knees and elbows against the rocky walls. He panicked, because it seemed so far that he thought he would never, never reach the end.

He listened, even while he was running, for footsteps

coming after him, for a sliding body or thrashing wings, or the hot, panting breath of a beast. But the only footsteps were his own, the sliding body was his too, pushing through the rocks, and the frantic breathing was his own fear and desperation.

All at once he was back in the cave where he had begun. The burst of sunshine coming through the crack seemed like a blessed shaft of light from Heaven, taking him by surprise.

He rushed out on to the shore, so relieved to be there that he panted for nearly five minutes before strolling back to the hut. The only thing that damped his relief was the memory of the awful state of the cave where he had left Jonathan Pickering's treasure.

All that night he dreamed he was going down endless flights of dark stairs. Each time he woke with a start he had not nearly reached the bottom. He sat up and sweated, but the moon pouring its light through the window showed him he was not in the cave, but lying on his bed in the hut. Really he had nothing to worry about at all.

But he did worry, and with daylight came a curiosity that haunted him all the day through. What was down at the bottom of that hole? Where did the steps lead to? How deep was the chamber under the earth? After all, with the slab pushed to one side there was nothing to close the gap if one were to climb down and look.

It was only his *thinking*, his feelings, his dread of something unknown and weird that had stopped him from climbing inside. Why should there be anything there to frighten him? And anyway, as a tenant, ought he really to leave the place in such a muddle?

That night his dreams were worse than ever.

In the morning he failed for the first time to put a stone in the tin, but hurried off to the cave when the sun was barely clear of the horizon. He hoped without admitting it that the crack might have vanished during the night, but it had not. It seemed to have been there for ever. Fate had left the way open to him. He walked straight through the crack and squeezed between the rocky walls, on and on and on into the heart of the hill.

He had no idea he had come so far only the day before yesterday. It seemed darker too, but maybe that was just his imagination. He felt rather braver, because he had brought with him a stout club, strong enough, he hoped, to lever the rocky lid back into place, and also weighty enough to protect him against anything evil coming up the stairs.

He hardly dared to look into the cavern when he reached it, but everything lay just as he remembered. The three stones, side by side, looked like a family of well-behaved sisters, and the massive rock slab seemed so enormous that he could not believe he had actually handled it alone.

He longed for his torch, left far away in his bedroom at home, beyond reach of his island life. He had a box of matches in his pocket, but to strike them was to light up only swirls of darkness and little else.

Paddy wedged the end of his club underneath the slab of rock, but hardly shifted it at all. This was awkward, because somehow or other he must get that awful hole covered up, and this time he knelt on the edge and peered down, with a fast-beating heart, to listen to the depths.

There was no movement at all down below. The cavern around him had lost some of its terrors. Paddy leaned far into the shadowy staircase and even put a foot over the edge to test the steps. They were rock solid.

Without much hope he pulled the first three stones across the gap, but the only thing that happened was the bouncing of the smallest stone on to the next stair, and its rapid rattling and galloping out of sight. Some way below it found a landing place and crashed to a halt.

At least it had not fallen into water!

Paddy was relieved to find there was a solid bottom to the stairs, but appalled at the same time to lose the stone that was such an important part of the treasure chamber. He would simply have to try to get it back again.

Nothing stirred, so clutching his club he crept into the hole and very cautiously descended the stairs, listening at every step as he went.

It grew darker and darker, yet as he climbed deeper into the earth it was not really dark at all. Some reflection from the dim light above penetrated the hole, and went with him to the bottom, where suddenly there were no more stairs, but a flat stone floor, and a round cavern with flat, rough rock walls.

Paddy struck a match and looked all about him, as far as the feeble light would carry. There was nothing at all but emptiness, and the fallen stone lying in the middle of the floor, waiting to be picked up.

He went all the way round the walls, striking matches. The walls were a little damp, but had no cracks or fissures. Dim as the light was, he could see nothing of any interest whatever, and anti-climax overwhelmed him.

All his imagined horrors faded away and all sense of fear evaporated. He was alone in a dull, empty old cave with nothing interesting in it at all.

He picked up the stone and trudged back up the stairs feeling deeply disappointed. Once he could tug or lever the stone back across the hole he would tidy up the place and leave it for good. He fairly romped up the last five steps.

This time he did not mean to be beaten by any old rock. He had moved it before and he would move it again. Even if it took him the rest of the day to shift it back inch by inch, shift it he would, and he attacked it with vigour.

To his surprise it was not so difficult after all. The slab slid forward in front of his club, shuffled across the sand and was slipping into place, when just for a split second Paddy saw below a flash of light, so brief but so vivid it reminded him of the gleam in his mother's ring when the sun caught it. Immediately he stopped pushing. The rock remained halfway across the opening.

Paddy lay on his front and peered down into the darkness. Nothing. And then again the briefest gleam of light, like the wink of an eye. But silence, a long, deep silence.

He got his head and shoulders through the gap till he was almost hanging upside down. And the very small, very flashing gleam of light flashed back at him out of the darkness on the opposite side of the cavern. It might, by some wonderful chance, be a jewel!

This time he was not afraid but only curious. He reversed his body, and squeezed down into the hole, which was only just large enough to take his body and legs. The edges were rocky, and it was quite plain that underneath the sand the entrance had been cut out of stone.

He was halfway down when it came to him that the rock might spitefully close over his head while he was there but he was too curious to worry. Instead, he dropped off the steps, crossed the floor in the nearly pitch darkness, and ran his hands over the rocks and the wall where he had seen the light gleaming.

He had no difficulty in finding it now. Low on the ground, round and small and no larger than a coat button, lay a pebble with an eye in it.

Paddy picked it up and handled it. The stone was so smooth and so creamy it was a delight to touch. He could not think how he had managed to miss it before. The eye in the middle gazed solemnly back at him. Why it had flashed and gleamed he could not imagine, for now it was quite dull and lustreless, though very beautiful when he struck a match to look at it. It was one of the strangest things he had ever found, and he could not bear to leave it behind, so he wrapped it in a corner of his handkerchief and climbed the stairs again.

This time the slab of rock obligingly gave way when he pushed it, and moved back again quite easily when he came to replace it over the stairs. On top of the rock he placed the largest of the three stones, and then the next, and finally the last. He filled in the spaces with sand, smoothed the sand about the stones, and by the time he left the cave looked neat and orderly.

Back down the long passage Paddy ran, and came out half-blinded into the sunshine on the shore.

He spread his handkerchief on the rocks, and looked with pleasure at the coloured pebble out of the depths of the cavern. It wasn't a jewel. It wasn't a relic. it was just a small, round, pretty stone, with the likeness of an eye in the middle.

But the eye had flashed at him—he could swear it. He cupped it in his hands, but there was no flashing now. One could hardly have pictured it as Jonathan Pickering's treasure. But Paddy had a peculiar pleasure in handling it. He put it away in his pocket feeling about ten times as happy as he had the day before.

7
The Great-Grandmother

Now he had the Pebble Paddy felt he had found a friend, almost a companion. He liked to roll it round the palm of his hand and to stroke it with his fingers. The eye in the middle was quite dim in the sunlight, but just once or twice it gleamed at him from the corner where he had made it a nest of leaves.

It had all been worth the journey down the winding passage, though why, he was quite unable to say. The Pebble was perfectly lifeless, and yet—somehow, it *was* alive! It felt valuable, but not in the way a jewel would feel of value. It felt personally valuable, which was altogether different.

He carried it with him everywhere, swimming, fishing, playing squash, cooking berries. Once he dropped it in a pool and spent ten agonising minutes searching for it among the little shells and limpets and cockles and stones.

When at last he found it he was nearly in tears. There was nothing, really, to cry about, yet he knew he wanted to keep it with him for ever. After finding it he raced about the island, tossing it in the air and pouncing on it where it fell. It was his all magnificent, all important, all inimitable Pebble. It became more important to him every day. It was *his*. He kept it in a corner of the rocks, like a shrine.

Some weeks after the cave incident the weather changed. Clouds began like specks in the sky, and grew to the size of umbrellas. Then they all joined up into a dark and dreary bank that covered the sun, and the rain began.

Paddy had not considered rain. It did not seem to belong to a desert island. He sat playing his mouth organ and waiting for the deluge to stop. But it did not stop. He played all the tunes he knew and still it rained. The rain painted a grey, wet veil across the island, underneath which the sea flopped black and lifeless, the little waves hardly troubling to break upon the shore. Against the rain the palm trees stood like lanky ghosts, drooping their branches that were glistening with water. The squash court was a swamp.

Paddy ate wet berries and sodden leaves when he became hungry enough to brave the rain. The leaves were like potato crisps that had been left out all night, and the berries had hardly any taste at all.

He wandered out in the drenching rain, got soaked, got cold, and retired shivering to the hut. There was rain in his mouth organ now, and he had simply nothing to do. He sat tossing his pebble from hand to hand and feeling bored. More bored at every minute. Almost unbearably bored.

'Perhaps this is the rainy season,' thought Paddy. 'Perhaps it will go on for days! But not, surely, for months?'

He lay on his bed, still holding the Pebble, and heard the fat drops of rain splashing through a hole in the roof on to the floor quite close to his pillow. He could not be bothered to avoid it.

He fell asleep, and woke to find himself clutching the same little piece of paper he had written on long ago, with the names on it of all the people he had least wanted to invite to share his island.

It was different now. Almost any of them would have been welcome to pay an afternoon call. Or longer for that matter if it was going to go on raining like this. Because there really was not a great deal for a boy to do alone, day after day on a desert island, for a whole year on end. Fishing, yes; playing squash, all right in a limited way; making music—so far so good, *but how long would it last*?

More than anything at that moment he admitted that he

wanted a television set. He sat on the edge of his bed and studied his list. Some of the names felt like ancestors:

'Aunt One.

Aunt Two . . . .'

Aunt One would have her violin, and they could play duets. Aunt Two would definitely make a garden, and maybe grow lettuce and strawberries . . . .

'Judy . . . .' It would be quite fun to have Judy on the island. There were so many things they could do together.

'The milkman.' No, probably not.

'Uncle Brett.' So soon got tired of cricket.

All right, any one of them for a few hours, but not to stay. Likewise his parents, though he would have been very glad to see them coming along just now. Very glad indeed.

He thought seriously about Judy, but then remembered that she was an avid television fan, and hated to miss a single programme of her choice. And when she could not have what she wanted she became impossible to live with and they always quarrelled. If only he had thought of bringing a television with him so many problems would be solved. Or some books. Why had he told Jonathan Pickering that he would not be wanting books? Of course he wanted books! Or a video, or tapes, or anything to tell him stories. And he remembered that the best storyteller in the world was his great-grandmother, Mrs Daisy Bucket, so no wonder he had not included her on his list.

Jonathan Pickering had said he could have only one companion at a time on the island, but he never said how he was to find a companion. Mere wishing would not bring one.

Just to prove it he held up the paper in the hand that was not clutching the Pebble and pronounced: 'I wish that my great-grandmother, Mrs Daisy Bucket, was here on the island to stay with me . . . .'

The little old lady in the doorway was shaking the rain off her umbrella before she came into the room.

'Rain before seven, fine before eleven!' said his great-grandmother, Mrs Daisy Bucket, wiping her feet on the sand as she entered. 'A pity it is so wet, dear, but I trust you are making yourself happy?'

Paddy could not answer for shock. He sat shaking on the bed, staring at his great-grandmother as if she were a ghost, which, for the moment, he fully believed her to be.

'You might give me a kiss, Patrick!' his great-grandmother said reproachfully. 'I came as soon as I got your invitation. It would be nice of you to make me welcome!'

Paddy flew into her arms and hugged her. She was as fat and solid as he had ever known her, and the familiar scent of lavender water and peppermints enveloped him from her clothes. She was his mother's grandmother, but she always seemed to have come out of the Ark.

'How did you get here and where are we?' Paddy asked her in excitement.

'Well you ought to know! It's your island, I believe!' said the old lady cheerfully. 'I really have no idea! But here I am, and here you are, and I believe the rain is on the point of stopping. I knew it couldn't go on for ever. Have you got a nice cup of tea?'

Paddy had not thought of tea since he came to the island. He had to admit this, shamefacedly, to his great-grandmother.

'Oh well,' she said, 'then we'll do without, but it seems rather a pity! Have you thought of boiling leaves? I've brought a little packet of Earl Grey with me, but I'm afraid it won't last long.'

'Did you bring anything else?' Paddy asked hopefully, for her bag looked very soft and squashy. No earthly good to hope she had thought of bringing a television set.

'Marmalade for breakfast,' she announced, 'and my mending materials. Oh yes, I brought some peppermints! Would you like one?'

After a diet of berries peppermints tasted like the food of the gods. Paddy sucked joyously.

'Shall we have a meal now?' Mrs Daisy Bucket asked. 'Soon it will have quite stopped raining, and you can show me all over your island. Where do you keep your food?'

Paddy pulled out the container that held the berries. It

was half full of water. The leaves, so delicious when dry, were sodden and grey.

'How disgusting!' said his great-grandmother cheerfully. 'Perhaps we had better explore first. I think the sun is coming out. You lead the way!'

Paddy led and she followed.

Already the damp was rising off the sands in a misty curtain of fog. Underneath it the sea was once again blue, while high above, the gulls tossed merrily in a sunny sky. The fog melted away before their eyes. The sand grew warm under their feet.

'Excuse me, I think I'll take off my shoes,' said Mrs Daisy Bucket. Leaning heavily on Paddy's shoulder she dropped first one shoe and then another, and rolled down her thick grey stockings.

'That feels better,' she said, flexing her toes in the sand. 'It reminds me of going to Margate when I was a girl.'

This had so often been the beginning of a colourful story that Paddy listened expectantly, but Great-Grandma was wholly taken up with the feel of the shore under her feet, and teetered along holding up her skirts and petticoats and squirming in delight as the small crabs and jellyfish wriggled between the toes of her pretty white feet.

By the time they had circled the island the berries on the bushes had dried, the leaves were once again crisp and tasty, and Paddy was able to offer her a tolerable meal.

'Well, well, when in Rome eat as Rome does!' said Mrs Daisy Bucket, taking large mouthfuls. 'And I must say you look very well on it! Milk? No! Sugar? No. Bread? No, of course not! Just berries, berries, berries! And it could be worse! Now, what about that bed and bedding? And all your clothes, and shoes and socks? We must get them all out and air them. And we'll move the bed where it won't be dripped on by the next shower. Come along!'

Soon the rocks were draped with blankets and clothing. The bed was pushed into a corner, and a fresh brew of berries was bubbling on the stove.

It no longer looked like Paddy's home, but it looked homely.

Mrs Daisy Bucket was dusting everything she could find with a torn pair of Paddy's shorts. After which she sat on a rock and told him endless stories. Each time she seemed likely to stop she went on again. Paddy thought it was much better than television.

As darkness fell it seemed only courteous to offer her the bed in the house and to sleep in the cave himself.

When he woke in the morning it was quite late, and he remembered that something nice had happened.

The something nice was his great-grandmother serving breakfast on a rock outside, over which her umbrella, wide open, presided like a summer parasol.

8
Great-Grandma on the Island

'What actually happened was this . . .' Paddy was telling his great-grandmother. 'I did not actually invite you—I was simply wishing for you, and you came!'

'When you are my age,' said Mrs Daisy Bucket, serving berries, 'it is very nice indeed to be wished for. But I imagine you have to be careful what you do wish for? Have you had much success up till now? It could be something to do with the atmosphere of the island. I don't care to presume, of course, but if you could see your way to wishing me some cornflakes?'

'Oh yes!' cried Paddy with enthusiasm.

'I wish for some cornflakes!' he announced with a flourish, but nothing appeared. 'You try!' he suggested.

Mrs Daisy Bucket closed her eyes and wished for cornflakes. She had no more success than Paddy.

'I'm very sorry,' Paddy apologised. 'It's a pity about the cornflakes, but on the other hand it seems to me we are doing very well just as we are.'

'Oh certainly, certainly,' agreed his great-grandmother. 'It is a beautiful island, and the berries are quite delicious. And I slept very well last night. Would you like a peppermint?'

When they had finished their peppermints they played French cricket with a piece of wood and a large round apple-like fruit that tasted horrid.

Then Paddy played all the tunes he knew on his mouth organ, and his great-grandmother applauded every one. He felt like a concert performer.

After that Mrs Daisy Bucket told him stories, and then it was dinnertime, after which they fished, and the day drifted on till it was time to go to bed again.

Paddy did slightly envy Mrs Daisy Bucket the one and only bed and blanket, but he curled up and slept well in a corner of the cave, while she, presumably, slept well inside the hut.

The squash court had dried, and in the morning he introduced his great-grandmother to the game. She took to it like a duck to water, and beat him in two straight sets. By now she was playing barefoot, and had tucked her voluminous petticoats into a large pair of pink bloomers.

At first Paddy thought this was funny, but then he felt a little ashamed of her, and hoped no ships passing by would pick her out on their telescope.

Presently she discarded the petticoats and ran about in a white blouse and the pink bloomers, with her white hair blowing in the wind. She seemed very happy and carefree, and she could run even faster than Paddy could.

It made her even better at games. She won at squash, she won at cricket, she won at French cricket. Then she was ashamed of herself and made mistakes on purpose. Paddy felt he was being treated like a little boy again and this made him very embarrassed. If she had not been his dearly-loved great-grandmother he would have come near to disliking her.

And she was beginning to take over the island—*his* island! Not only was she sleeping in the hut, but she was treating it as her own property—decorating it with shells and island flowers; making a little garden outside the door; draping the bed with the blanket folded all fancy-wise.

When another tropical storm drove them indoors Paddy hardly knew the place. All his clothes had been laundered—washed in the stream and ironed with a hot flat stone.

Mrs Daisy Bucket took over the cooking and the timing of the meals.

When he went fishing loud cries as well as delicious smells brought him galloping back to eat. She even cooked his fish for him, and he had to admit she did it very much better than he did.

She was so kind and loving he could not complain but it was not really very *convenient* having her always about the place, and not knowing how long she was going to stay, or how he could possibly tell her to go. She seemed so happy, she did not seem to want to go home at all.

Almost at once he had asked for news of his parents.

'Did they miss me?' he wanted to know.

'They think you are staying with me!' said his great-grandmother. 'And your father has just been offered a post in America for a few months, so they asked me to look after you meanwhile. It has all worked out very well.'

Paddy would have preferred to be a bit more missed. He brooded a little, and then decided to write them a letter. His pencil was still fresh, and the lead fairly long. All that he needed was paper and a postman.

Finally he wrote, quite briefly, on the peppermint bag, ending with lots of love, and just saying that he and his great-grandmother were well, and the weather was fine.

'Sometimes we have a dreadful storm . . . ' he added.

But there was no postman to collect it. Then they found an old green bottle under the step of the hut.

'Perfect!' said Mrs Daisy Bucket. 'That is the way letters are always sent abroad from islands.'

They launched it together, and watched the bottle with the letter in it bobbing gently away from the shore.

By morning it was gone.

'When do you think it will get to them?' Paddy wanted to know, but his great-grandmother was unable to tell him.

'There's one thing—with your home address on it someone will quickly forward it to America!' she said.

Paddy felt very far away from his parents indeed.

9
Still on the Island

Paddy and his great-grandmother did their best to explain the granting of Paddy's wish, and the chances of having another one. They never associated it with the Pebble, which lay deserted in the corner of Paddy's handkerchief, carefully hidden behind a rock.

They hunted everywhere else for clues. Paddy sat exactly where he had sat to make the wish come true. He even waited for a shower of rain and did it then. He wished harmless wishes for cornflakes and packets of tea, but nothing happened. By now he had quite forgotten he had once wanted a television set. His great-grandmother tried too, but without success.

Mrs Daisy Bucket took to wandering off into the bushes of the island and choosing her own berries. One day she woke up really ill. Paddy did not know what to do for her, and was terrified. His great-grandmother had been sick all night and was quite blue in the face.

'You mustn't worry, dear,' she told him in a feeble voice, 'I shall get over it by and by....'

But meanwhile she was suffering terrible stomach pains and being sicker and sicker.

Paddy remembered that Jonathan Pickering had told him illness could be cured by good berries, but which berries were good and which were bad? He flew off into the bushes with a large shell to put them in.

When be came back his great grandmother was scarcely breathing.

He carried five or six different berries in the shell. Mrs Daisy Bucket picked them over with a feeble hand.

'Not these, dear—they are very pretty, but those are the

ones that made me so ill. And those pink ones taste horrible! The yellow ones make your teeth ache, they can't do you any good! Those blue ones *might* be of use! Aie—eee! They give me the most terrible pains! I think I'm dying, Patrick, I really do! Oh what will become of me?'

Paddy was so desperate he crushed all the rest of the berries together and crammed them into her mouth. After a moment or two her colour came back and she began to lick her lips.

'That's better,' she said in quite her normal voice. 'How clever of you, Patrick, to know which of the berries would cure me! Which were they?'

Paddy did not know. He had frantically mixed the remaining berries all together, and his great-grandmother had swallowed the lot.

'Don't worry, dear, it was all my fault!' Mrs Daisy Bucket said. 'I had no business to go about tasting strange fruits. I hope you *never* do! It is extremely dangerous. I might have died! And I really can't think how you could have buried me! It was a very, very unwise thing to do. I might have lain here for *weeks* . . . .'

'Oh no! Oh no, Grandma, I could easily have buried you!' protested Paddy. 'I'd have pulled you by the feet and . . . .'

'Don't be so unfeeling!' snapped his great-grandmother sharply. 'I am very hungry now, and I would like some of your ordinary berries and some leaves. And a long drink of cold spring water. Please fetch it for me, and then I will leave my bed.'

Mrs Daisy Bucket spent the next few days making herself a grass skirt and a broad-brimmed hat from palm leaves, and now that she had a hat over her white hair and a skirt to hide her pink bloomers she looked quite normal, even though her vest was old-fashioned, and not at all like a blouse.

She resigned herself to eating ordinary berries, and she still won every game they played together, but she no longer seemed very happy. Paddy did all he could to amuse her, but it was obvious that she was not particularly satisfied with the desert island.

'Well, there isn't very much to do, is there?' she said pettishly, in answer to his anxious questions. 'I can put up with the food, but I would enjoy a woman's magazine, or some knitting, or some real cooking to do. I've mended all you clothes and my own. There's nothing else I *can* mend! I don't know how long I've been here, but it seems at least a year and a half! My plants won't grow! The bed is terribly hard at night! And I would so much enjoy a cup of real tea!'

This outburst from his great-grandmother was so unlike her that it disturbed Paddy greatly. He knew she had not been more than a few weeks on the island, but it seemed unkind to point this out. He was beginning, too, to wish himself alone again. A discontented companion was worse than none at all. And by now he was tired of being spring-cleaned and mended for and cooked for and told when to come and eat.

Mrs Daisy Bucket was anxious to get home before the Church Bazaar.

Paddy still enjoyed her stories, but he was getting tired of hearing them over and over again.

At last they decided together that it might be better if they lived on different sides of the island. Then they could go to tea with each other, or to dinner, or even to breakfast, but they need not see each other all the time.

Mrs Daisy Bucket suggested that he should build a hut, and came to help him do it. Together they lugged driftwood and palm fronds, and made a kind of wigwam. It looked quite smart from the outside, but the flies liked it too, and buzzed in and out all night, till his great-grandmother lent him her discarded petticoats to drape over the doorway, and then the flies stayed outside.

It was terribly hot, but it was flyproof, and Paddy felt private again.

He enjoyed calling, 'Goodnight!' to his great-grandmother and walking off across the island at night after tea and a session of storytelling.

He refused to admit to himself that Mrs Daisy Bucket now had all his previous territory. She had his hut and his squash court and his cave and his rocks and his fishing pools. The fishing wasn't nearly so good on this side of the island, neither was the view. He no longer had the sunset, nor the lookout to the point where any rescuing ship was likely to appear. But she was very good to him, and had been a very great help with the tent, and every now and again she brought over a large platter of cooked food, and she had given him more than half his share of the matches.

10
The Pirate Ship

One morning Paddy awoke to the sound of voices. Not the echoes of the dreams he often had, but real voices calling and shouting, and his great-grandmother's voice answering high and clear.

He leapt up and raced across the island in the early morning sunshine, his heart beating so loudly he hardly had the breath left to run with.

Had people—*real* people—landed on the shore? Was it being overrun by strangers that he could not drive away? The closer he came to the hut and his little bay the louder and shriller became the voice of Mrs Daisy Bucket.

When the trees thinned out he saw to his intense astonishment the sails, masts and outline of a great schooner at anchor just off the shore. At some time during the night it had stolen round the point, and was now moored opposite to the hut, while six or eight villainous-looking pirates were lowering a boat off the side and preparing to get into it and row ashore.

On the sand, complete in grass skirt, vest and palm leaf hat, his great-grandmother was shaking her fist and shouting threats at them, brandishing in one hand the stick she used for cooking, and in the other the board Paddy had written on to show that the island was private property.

High on the topmast of the schooner, to Paddy's horror, he recognised the skull and crossbones of a pirate galleon, and within seconds he was standing at his great-grandmother's side and adding his own threats and curses to her screams.

On the bridge, looking down at them with dark disdain, stood a figure with arms crossed upon his chest. One eye

was covered by a black patch, and his air of dignity and authority showed him to be the pirate captain himself.

Paddy stepped forward into the shallow water and held up his hand. 'STOP!' he shouted. 'You can't come here! This island is private!' He added for good measure: 'It is private all over!'

'Oh yes?' jeered the pirates, now taking their places in the boat. 'Who does it belong to then?'

'To *me*!' shouted Paddy, stamping one foot so that the

water splashed up over his head. 'It is my private island for one year! I have a contract to say so!'

The captain came to the rail of the bridge. 'Who gave you the contract, young mister?' he shouted.

'Mr Jonathan Pickering!' Paddy bawled back.

The sailors in the boat shipped the oars they were handling and looked up at their captain.

'To Jonathan Pickering, does it?' he repeated with some interest. 'Oho, yes! To Jonathan Pickering!'

He left the bridge and reappeared quite shortly just above the sailors on the rail of the boat. 'Steady on, men! No hurry! Nothing to lose by waiting! And do you know Mr Jonathan Pickering, young mister?'

'Yes I do!' said Paddy stoutly. 'And he promised me that terrible things would happen if more than two people came on this island at once! He has rented it to *me*!'

He noticed a shiver going through the waiting sailors, pirates being very superstitious.

'And who is this lady?' the captain asked more pleasantly. 'Did you find her on the island when you came here?'

'No I did not!' said Paddy indignantly. 'This is my great-grandmother, Mrs Daisy Bucket, who has come on a visit to cook for me . . . .'

'*Cook*!' came a roar of delight from the pirates in the boat. 'Why, we've been all over the Spanish main looking for a cook! Ask her if she will come and cook for us!'

Paddy stole a glance at his great-grandmother, expecting a withering glance of scorn, but to his surprise she was looking quite excited.

The pirate captain was looking at her too.

'Well, madam,' he said to her politely, 'did you hear the offer? Would you like to come and cook for us pirates as my men suggest?'

Mrs Daisy Bucket looked coy.

'What are the conditions like?' she asked, but Paddy could see she was bubbling with excitement.

'Come and see for yourself, madam,' the captain invited her. 'Don't worry, boy! We'll bring her back if she doesn't want to stay! But if she does . . . ' he cackled back over his shoulder as he handed Mrs Daisy Bucket on to the ship a few minutes later, 'why we can find a place for *you* here as well, I expect!'

The pirates were now in an exceedingly good humour.

They rowed quietly up and down the bay while inside the galleon Paddy's great-grandmother was being shown round the kitchen and the storerooms and was gasping with joy and enthusiasm at everything she saw.

Tea—the hold was stacked with boxes of tea.

Cornflakes! Enough to last a regiment for a whole year!

Chocolate! Raisins, oranges, nuts, grapefruit, crystallised cherries, biscuits, bananas, two dear little monkeys and a baby parrot. And the kitchens were as modern and as up-to-date as design could make them. Also the most beautiful cook's apron and hat were hanging on pegs behind the door.

Set around the kitchen in great bins were pounds and pounds of flour, wheat, rice, and every kind of cereal. The whole place, though modern beyond all dreams, was in dire need of a wash down, and this appealed to Mrs Daisy Bucket more than all the stores put together.

One of the crew hastened to make her a cup of tea, and it was all she could do not to accept the situation offered to her there and then. Instead, she stalled a little.

'I have never considered becoming a cook to a pirate ship . . . ' she said, gently slurping her tea, while waves of delight passed down her throat.

'Madam, I truly believe that at this moment you will be the only pirate lady cook in the whole world. If you accept the situation, that is,' said the Captain, lounging up against the sink. 'My men will make so much of you! I shall treat you as the ship's First Lady! You will have a free hand to provide, not only daily food, but feasts and banquets when we take our prizes. You shall have the privilege of providing the last meal for those unfortunate prisoners forced to walk the plank . . . .'

'Walk the plank?' repeated Mrs Daisy Bucket faintly.

'So rare! So very rare!' the captain said. 'And when they

do, they always deserve it. Please have another cup of tea, dear madam, and then we must take you ashore, because your young grandson will be getting anxious.'

Mrs Daisy Bucket could not speak for the moment. She longed, even *craved* to accept this amazing offer and sail away as cook to the pirate ship, but how to leave her precious great-grandson on the island alone?

If Paddy agreed to come too, then everything would resolve itself, and the dreadful diet of berries would become a thing of the past—but if he did not?

'You must give me time to think it over, Captain,' she murmured, impressed in spite of herself by his honesty and frankness. 'I must talk it over first with—with the tenant of the island, and see what he thinks about it . . . .'

Paddy was waiting impatiently on the sands when Mrs Daisy Bucket left the boat and paddled the last few metres to the shore. She said goodbye to the crew and the captain saluted her from the bridge.

'He looks as if he owns you, Great-Grandma!' said Paddy jealously.

'Oh no! Oh no!' said Mrs Daisy Bucket hastily. She realised she had forgotten to bring any provisions for Paddy, and there had been such a choice in the hold of the ship. She felt very ashamed of herself for not asking, and began to describe to him all the wonders of the ship's kitchen and storehouses.

'Everything you can think of to eat,' she told him. 'And they tell me I can plan the meals every day, just as I please! They would like you to be their kitchen boy, and that would give you just the same privileges as myself, or very nearly! We have to make up our minds by sundown, when they sail away. What do you think about it, dear?'

Paddy's answer was to wander away alone to his cave. He sat there brooding for several hours while ideas flitted in and out of his head.

At one moment the excitement of living on a pirate ship filled his mind, and he decided he must and should go with his great-grandmother, but at the next minute his heart sank low, as he imagined himself at the beck and call of all the rough sailors, being cursed by the pirate captain, pushed about by the crew, confined below decks when the wind and the sea called him aloft, and never, never again his own master.

He regretted the inevitable parting with his great-grandmother, Mrs Daisy Bucket. She had been good to him even if she was bossy, but it really might be better to let her go, and to live by himself again. This island no longer held the delights he had once enjoyed, but it was better to be his own boss than to be driven about by all these older people.

He went to his tent to fetch his mouth organ, and found the coverings gone from the structure. While he had been brooding in the cave his great-grandmother had stripped away her petticoats and skirt, and left it empty.

Back on the shore she was packing up her clothes from the hut. It all looked terribly final, like somebody leaving home for good.

'I'm sorry, dear,' she said, on seeing his face, 'but time was getting on, and I thought if you had made up your mind to say no, we could easily put them all back again!'

Paddy felt betrayed, but he said nothing. He walked down to the shore and waved to the pirate ship. Soon a little boat was lowered into the water, manned by two lusty pirates. They rowed to the shallow water near the shore, and Paddy handed his great-grandmother into a seat in the bows. She turned to help him in after her, but he shook his head violently.

'I'm not coming,' Paddy said.

Before she could change her own mind the two pirates

rowed Mrs Daisy Bucket back to the ship. When they handed her up the gangplank Paddy could see that she was crying.

Paddy stood for a long time watching the preparations for the ship's departure. Once the captain himself waved to him from the bridge. And presently in the dusk the little rowing boat left the galleon's side and stole towards the shore. The same two sailors were at the oars.

Paddy stiffened. Did they mean to kidnap him after all?

He picked up a stick, to defend himself, but secretly decided to run if they came after him. Better wait, however, to see what they wanted, and if the large bundle they carried in the bows meant anything at all.

And it did, too. It was a large box wrapped in a tarpaulin, and when they were some metres from the beach the two sailors heaved it overboard, and silently rowed back to the ship.

The package came bobbing towards him. Paddy pulled it on to the sands and the very smell of it was good. It was full to the very brim with delicious things to eat, especially oranges and chocolate.

11
The Pebble

Underneath all the good things to eat Paddy found a piece of paper. Written on it were the words: 'With fond love from Great-Grandma.'

Darkness had fallen on the island. The moon was a mere slice in the sky.

Paddy made several journeys to and from the shore, carrying his bounty to the cave. There were not so many flies on this side of the island, but he felt it was safer, just the same, to put all the eatables in the cave where there were no flies at all. Neither had he seen there any mice or other creatures that might help themselves to his new provisions.

All the while he kept an eye on the shadowy outline of the pirate galleon that was busy casting off to sea. Faint cries and orders came over the water. Small and then larger waves rolled into the shore as the great ship up-anchored and cast away.

Once he thought he heard his name called, and ran to the edge of the water to see if his great-grandmother had

changed her mind and wanted to come back to him.

He called to her at the top of his voice: 'Grandma! Great-Grandma! Are you there?'

But the cry that came back to him was quite firm and resolute: 'Goodbye, Patrick dear! Goodbye!'

He could not see her, but he pictured her standing on the bridge in the vast, shadowy bulk of the disappearing schooner. He waved till the shadow was part of the night, and had vanished round the point of the island.

Paddy wandered back to the hut, now completely cleared of Mrs Daisy Bucket's possessions, but still smelling faintly of peppermints and lavender water. The bed had been pulled back into its old position. There was a little pile of mended clothes on the floor beside it, and the blanket was neatly folded on top of the mattress. On top of the blanket, wrapped in a small leaf, were five peppermints.

When he thought of all the good things piled up inside the cave this touched Paddy deeply, and a lump rose up in his throat.

He lay down on the bed, but sleep would not come, and presently he left the tidy hut to finish the night in the cave. Already his great-grandmother seemed a long, long way away.

In the morning there was nobody to greet him, and while he was putting away his clothes in the hut the Pebble dropped out of his shorts on to the floor.

'I suppose I shall have to say Good Morning to *you* now!' he addressed it angrily.

'Good morning!' the Pebble replied. 'I must say, it is polite of you to take the trouble to say a word to me after all these weeks! Never, not once have you spoken to me since you found me! Used me, oh yes, but not personally. Don't apologise! It's your loss, not mine!'

Paddy was too flabbergasted to answer.

'I do beg your pardon!' he said after a short pause, clutching the Pebble so as not to drop it on the floor. 'I really—that is—I mean I had almost forgotten all about you while my great-grandmother was here.'

'I know,' agreed the Pebble. 'You thought I was just a *thing*! Well, so I am. But even things have feelings . . . .'

'I suppose they do,' said Paddy in shame, remembering how he had treated the Pebble, and never spoken directly to it. If he had, what would have happened?

'I mean—*are* you Mr Jonathan Pickering's treasure?' he asked, balancing it on the open palm of his hand, now that he had almost stopped trembling. 'He never told me exactly what his treasure was,' Paddy went on, 'only that he wanted it looked after by whoever rented the island. If I had gone with my great-grandmother to work for the pirates, I would have taken you with me, I promise!'

The stone gave a little wriggle.

'I should not have gone!' it said firmly. 'I should have thrown myself into the water before they could get at me. They know very well that Mr Pickering has treasure on one of these islands, and one day they are going to find out which island it is. I have no doubt the old lady will tell them.'

'But she doesn't *know*!' cried Paddy, horrified.

'No? Are you sure? Didn't you tell her?' jeered the Pebble.

'I—I—not really! I never thought of it till Great-Grandma said you might be a wishing-stone!' said Paddy. 'But she wished for cornflakes and tea and sugar, and nothing ever came . . . .'

'*Never*?' asked the Pebble. 'Never at all?'

'Oh!' exclaimed Paddy, remembering the pirate ship, 'Well not for ages afterwards. We had forgotten all about it by then. We never thought it was *you*! Do you mean I can wish for just *anything?*' At once his thoughts turned to the provisions piled up inside the cave, so many of them and so varied that he could not think of anything left to wish for. Not even a television really.

'Of course!' said the Pebble. Its tone became just a little sly. 'There is only one thing I ought to warn you . . . .'

'What?' asked Paddy sharply. 'Jonathan Pickering never warned me about anything. Just that I couldn't have more than one other person on the island at the same time. He didn't even tell me where the island is. Do *you* know?'

'No. And it really doesn't matter,' the Pebble said. 'It's fair enough about not too many people at once. You see, if a lot of people came and they all had wishes something would have to go bust. As it is, each person can have just three wishes. Your great-grandma might have got her tea and her cornflakes and even her knitting, if she'd had the manners, but that would have left her nothing to get home with, if that pirate ship had not turned up when it did.'

Paddy shuddered, but his mind was racing on to calculate how many more wishes he had left for himself. Thankfully he realised he had only used one—on Great-Grandma.

'Could you possibly tell me,' he asked the Pebble, 'how many weeks I've been here? It's not a year yet, is it?'

'You have been on this island three months, two weeks, three days and nine hours,' said the Pebble. 'Also a few minutes—about seventeen actually. Don't you keep any account of the time?'

'I did once,' Paddy admitted, 'but by and by I forgot. The time is going very quickly! I thought it was awful when Great-Grandma left, but already it seems quite a lot better. I should love to have you around for conversation, but it's just a bit dangerous, in case I should have a wish while you were in my hand. I suppose I have actually to say the wish aloud?'

'Oh you do, you do!' agreed the Pebble. 'And there is always the risk of making a wish by mistake. I've seen it done. Poor old Jonathan Pickering did it himself! There he was, hiding me in the cavern, but he still had his hand on me when he said: "How I wish I could have a spell away from this dump!" And of course that's what he's doing now! If you want to be sure of staying here you had better put me back in the cave and just come and use me when you need to. How many wishes have you got left? Two? That should last you all right. Keep one up your sleeve. You never know when you may need it. You still have one left to play with.'

Paddy was thinking deeply. 'I've got sort of used to having someone around,' he said reluctantly, 'and after Great-Grandma I do seem to want some kind of companion. I wouldn't mind being alone for just a little while, but I do wish I had someone I could do things with—someone like Judy for instance . . . .'

He was tossing the Pebble up in the air as he spoke.

'If that's what you want!' said the Pebble sarcastically.

'Oh I'm sorry! That was a narrow squeak!' said Paddy, aghast.

He looked all round to see if by some awful chance his wish had been granted. There was no sign of anybody else on the island, not like his great-grandmother, who had materialised at once. With luck the Pebble had been in mid-air while he spoke.

Greatly relieved, he padded across the sand to the cave, and once there he thought he would put it, for really safe keeping, deep inside the hill at the far end of the passage.

He squeezed through the crack in the rocks and down the long twilit way. It seemed years since he had been there before, and the passage never seemed any shorter.

'I hope you don't mind,' he addressed the Pebble in his

pocket. 'I shall come and talk to you now and again and tell you what is going on. But I do feel you are safer here, don't you?'

The Pebble said nothing.

Paddy came to the far chamber, where he hesitated, but the fright he had given himself spurred him on. If he buried the Pebble just where he had found it, and covered up the hole and put the slab back, and the next stone and the next and the next, then he would be safe until he really needed it again.

This time the stones came up quite easily.

At the bottom of the steps Paddy apologised again to the Pebble: 'I'm so sorry to hide you away like this,' he said as he placed it in position. 'I shan't leave you for very long. You don't mind, do you?'

'Not at all,' the Pebble said politely.

Paddy saw the eye winking at him out of the darkness as he climbed up the steps. This time he left the smaller stones lying beside the big one outside the hole.

Then he hurried back along the passage to the cave, and found Judy unwrapping all the exciting parcels that his great-grandmother had sent him from the pirate ship.

12
Judy and the Cave

Judy greeted him with a beaming face. 'How lovely to see you again! I knew you would miss me! Do look at all these gorgeous things—your great-granny knows just what I like best!'

Paddy's mouth watered at the display of goodies, such as he had not seen in weeks. And he was pleased to see Judy. He knew he was. Only now he was left with only one single wish to last him nearly nine months, and that was a frightening thought. The least slip, and he would have to endure her for better or worse for all the rest of his time on the island.

He helped himself to a large and juicy orange.

'Have you seen my parents lately?' he asked carelessly.

'They are in America. They sent you a postcard,' Judy said, fishing in her pocket for a crumpled card. 'Your aunts send their love. They think you are on a visit to your great-granny. No, I don't know a bit where we are. I hoped you did!'

'Nobody ever tells me,' he grumbled, 'but it doesn't much matter.'

He was reading his parents' postcard, with their loves and messages on it. It was evident that they had not got his. The Statue of Liberty looked very unreal. And the aunts were so far away he had almost forgotten about them.

'Do they still play the violin?' he murmured.

'What, your parents? Or do you mean your Aunty Jay? Yes she does—all the time, and it drives my parents crazy! And your gardening aunty—guess what she did! She emptied all her weeds over the wall at the bottom of your garden into our vegetable patch! Can you believe it?'

Paddy could.

'What happened?' he asked.

'The most frightful, almighty, blazing father-and-mother of a row you ever heard!' said Judy dramatically, flinging wide her arms and spitting out orange pips. 'My dad on one side of the wall and your aunty on the other. Your other aunty arrived to join in, and my mum came rushing down to help my dad, and they all yelled and screamed. I thought it was really funny! At last my dad said he wouldn't tell the police if your aunty picked up all the weeds, and took them away again, and your aunty said well, she would, only she'd do it after dark, and she did, with your other aunty making such a noise on her violin with all the windows open that there's a row about that going on now! Only our dog howls till you can't hear yourself speaking, and your aunties are cross about that!'

'I suppose the violin makes him howl?' said Paddy hopefully.

'Well no, not really! You would think so, wouldn't you?' said Judy. 'But the funny thing is, our dog howls when the violin is *not* playing, and stops when your aunty begins! So there's all that to complain about too! You wouldn't believe it!'

Paddy and Judy began to laugh, and they rolled about laughing and sucking oranges and helping themselves to more.

'I'm glad you've come,' Paddy said between sucks. 'My great-grandma was lovely most of the time, but you know, she's so *old*! And she took my hut for a bedroom and changed it all so that honestly I didn't know it was mine! I suppose you'll have to have it for yours now,' he added with his face falling. 'I hadn't thought of that!'

'Let's have a look at it,' Judy suggested, and they went along the shore.

The hut still smelled faintly of peppermints, and still looked just a little bit like Mrs Daisy Bucket. But Paddy did not want to leave Judy to sleep in the cave. For one thing, she was slighter than he, and he feared she might slip off through the crack in the rock and find her way down the corridor to the treasure chamber at the end. He knew he had not left the stones as he had found them, and if Judy found the Pebble with the eye in it anything might happen.

But at the moment the worst thing would be for her to wish herself away again and leave him alone, for moment by moment he was becoming more glad of her company.

'We'll both sleep in the hut,' Judy decided. 'I'll have the bed and you can have the mattress. I don't mind it being hard, but I don't like island creepy-crawlies. And we'll each have a window of our own.'

'The blanket . . . ' Paddy began

'Cut it in half,' said Judy.

With her sharp teeth she had ripped it at the hem before he could protest. Within five minutes the one room house had become a two-bedded cottage. They agreed to eat on the shore.

Judy sat down to make weird noises on Paddy's mouth organ, while Paddy went off to fish from the rocks. He felt happy again, and quite sure he had found the right companion for the rest of his tenancy.

Judy cooked his fish, and later he showed her all round the island, just as he had shown his great-grandmother all those weeks ago.

'When I have time I will repair your tent,' she told him. 'I can use the tarpaulin that came round all those goodies your great-granny sent us.'

'We don't need the tent now,' said Paddy.

'We may if we quarrel,' Judy said sagely. 'It is always better to have somewhere to sulk in.'

'Where does the crack go to?' she asked when they were in the cave. Nothing escaped her sharp eyes.

'Oh. Just into the hill,' Paddy said. 'It's not safe there, as a matter of fact.'

'How much not safe?' asked Judy, interested.

She was fitting her slim body between the rocks.

Paddy pulled her away.

'Not a bit not safe!' he said urgently. 'The hill could fall in and bury you, halfway down . . . .'

'Have you tried?' asked Judy,

'Yes.'

'And did it?'

'No.'

'Well then!' said Judy. She disappeared inside. 'It goes on ever so far,' she told Paddy just as he was panicking that she would not return. 'Shall we go in together and see what happens?'

'NO!' said Paddy fiercely. 'I know it's not safe! I know we oughtn't to. We're *not* to go!'

Judy had come out now. She stared at him. 'You're not afraid of caves, are you?' she said.

'No of course I'm not!' he said crossly. 'I've been in far worse ones than this!'

'Then why get into such a state? Don't you want to know what is at the other end?'

'Not particularly,' Paddy said indifferently. 'Anway, I'm going to eat some chocolate.'

Judy came at once.

'You make it seem so important,' she grumbled. 'I don't want to go through the silly old crack any more than you do.'

But she did, and lying awake in the hut Paddy worried about the Pebble and the stones and the flight of steps going down—down—down—He didn't much mind Judy getting as far as the cavern, but its secrets she must not find.

Judy was such a sharp girl. She always found out everything she set her mind on. In the morning she was still going on about the crack and the passage behind it.

'Look here,' said Paddy severely. 'I don't know if you realise it, but the island doesn't belong to us.'

'Oh I know *that*!' said Judy. 'It belongs to Mr Jonathan Pickering. You told me . . . .'

'Wait!' said Paddy. 'So it does, but I have signed a contract to rent it for a year, and that makes me the owner for the whole of that time. Do you get it?'

'So what?' said Judy. 'That doesn't mean that I can't breathe here and swim, and play music, and—and dance!' She whirled away across the sands like a bright butterfly, with Paddy after her.

'What I mean is . . . ' he bawled in her ear, 'that I pay the rent and I'm boss here—see?'

'What rent do you pay?' she said, stopping her dance.

'I don't know yet. But it's not more than five pounds,' said Paddy reluctantly.

'Haven't you paid it yet? Then you're not boss at all!' laughed Judy. 'And I'll go in the cave whenever I like! I'll go *now*!'

He caught her and held her fast by the hair.

'All right—you go!' he hissed. 'All by yourself! I shan't help you even if you scream! It's horrid in there! I've *been*! Look,' he said suddenly, 'I've got an idea! We'll go next Wednesday. I'll take you myself. Will that do?'

'Oh yes,' she said, surprisingly meekly, 'but when is next Wednesday?' Neither of them knew.

'Say today is Monday,' Paddy said, 'and we'll drop a stone in the tin. Wednesday is the day after tomorrow. Will you wait till then?' He gave her head a little shake.

'Ow yes! All right, yes! Ouch! Let go my hair! Yes, I

promise. I won't go without you, Paddy. LET GO!'

He taught her how to play squash. Now at last he had an adversary that he could beat. And Judy did not seem to mind his winning every other game.

All the afternoon they fished and played squash and slept on the sand, and built beautiful villages among the rocks.

They were both exhausted, but no sooner was Judy asleep than Paddy slipped off his mattress, jumped out of the window and ran off to the cave.

It wasn't only the inner chamber that worried him, it was the lack of the Pebble. Safe enough it might be in its rocky fastness, but he missed its solidity and its wisdom. He found he kept clasping and unclasping his fingers as if he were holding it, and he wanted to be sure it was still where he left it. He did not want Judy to find it first, or even to know it was there. He wanted to be its sole owner, and to hide it now somewhere so completely safe and secure that nobody else could possibly discover it.

But he had not realised how unnerving it would be all alone in that dark corridor at night. He had no torch, no light from the sun, only the faintest glimmer from the moon.

It was so far, so much further than he remembered, that presently his nerve gave out, and he leaned against the wall shivering with terror and wondering why he had been such a fool as to argue Judy out of going by herself. She would never have dared to go so far without him. The Pebble would have been perfectly safe. There was nothing to worry about, no need to go and re-arrange the stones. No need to go any further at all . . . .

With a sigh of relief he began to retreat, but at the first bend he stopped, and called back softly in the darkness of the passage: 'Pebble! Are you there?'

It was still too far, maybe much too far, to get an answer, yet he thought he heard one.

Far, far away came a whisper, it was no more than that: 'Paddy! I'm here!'

He tried again, but heard no more.

Still, the reply had been positive. The Pebble was alive and expecting him—waiting for him down the long, dark stairs under the stone, and not so very far away . . . .

Behind him his bed waited, and the nearby company of Judy, sleeping sweetly in the island hut.

Ahead of him the weird Pebble, his companion, his wishing friend. A little dangerous, but also wise and helpful. He just wanted to talk to it.

'I needn't hold it,' he decided, 'and if I do I'll never say "I wish" again. Not, maybe, till the very last day of my year.'

He turned back and shuffled on towards the cavern.

13
Down in the Cavern

The last part of the corridor was shorter than he had expected. Suddenly he was in the final round chamber, with its circular rocky walls, and the stones lying side by side in the middle. He nearly fell into the shaft of the staircase before he knew where he was going.

'Pebble!' he shouted, half in fear, half in question, and from quite near him, but down below his feet came the Pebble's voice: 'I'm here, Paddy, I'm here!'

'Are you all right?' Paddy asked feebly.

It was such a silly thing to say, but nothing else came into his head. An amused little giggle came from below.

'Yes of course I'm all right!' said the Pebble. 'What about you? Are you getting lonely?'

'Well, sort of,' he admitted, 'but that's not it. I've got a friend come to stay. You must know it!' he blazed angrily. 'You brought her—you know you did!'

'Mmm,' said the Pebble.

Paddy could just see the eye gleaming in the dark as he hung over the edge of the hole.

'She wants to come down here,' Paddy said.

'What—already?' said the Pebble, surprised. 'Have you told her about me, then?'

'No, of course I haven't! And that's the point. I don't want her to find you. You belong to Mr Jonathan Pickering. And to *me*.'

'That's right,' said the Pebble.

'So I wanted to make sure you were still here, and to hide you—well a bit more safely, if you see what I mean, and to close down the slab and put the stones on top like they were before—and then she'll never find out you are here at all.'

The Pebble made a contemptuous snort.

'With your footmarks all over the cavern and all round the stones in the middle?' it scoffed. 'You'll be lucky if you manage it. That girl Judy is very quick and sharp. She puts two and two together while everybody else is making three. You won't find her coming down here without matches . . . .'

'Well then, can't I hide you a bit better?' Paddy asked desperately.

'All right,' said the Pebble, 'only you will have to come down here yourself to do it, I can't move by myself, you know!'

Paddy put one foot into the hole and felt for the steps. He followed it with the other toe. It was horribly dark down there.

'If only it was daylight,' he muttered. 'Oh I do wish I had brought some matches.'

'Look out!' said the Pebble sharply. 'Don't be so quick with your wishes! You may regret it if you go on like that. Come along, you are doing fine. There are twelve steps and they go straight down—that's it—five, six, seven! On you come, you're nearly there!'

Above all Paddy dreaded letting go of the top of the hole in the floor, which showed up dimly as he descended. The only comfort was that at each step the gleam of the Pebble shone brighter, and he felt less alone.

If the stone closed, horribly, above him, he would still have company. And he would still have one wish left. He could wish himself home again if he wanted to—away from the Pebble, away from Judy, back in his own house—*with the aunts, with school in the morning, with no parents there* . . . . He hit the ground while he thought he still had two steps to go.

'Well done,' said the Pebble. 'You are really a very brave

boy. Shake hands! And remember—no random wishing!'

Paddy picked up the Pebble. It was almost warm, and felt very friendly and reassuring.

'I'm so very glad to see you again,' Paddy said sincerely, 'I have missed you terribly.'

'Ah,' said the Pebble, 'company is company, but there's nothing quite like myself. Now, what are you going to do next?'

Paddy looked round in the pitch darkness, not that there was anywhere to look.

'Just supposing Judy got here,' he said, 'I'm wondering where we could hide you. You see, it's really very good fun having her to stay, but I don't want any accidents. I don't want to wish her away by mistake, or for her to do something of the sort to me.'

'That's just it,' said the Pebble. 'You probably realise that Judy has the right to three wishes too, while she is here. But, if I am correct in thinking, *you* only have one left? So that makes things a little awkward! So long as she doesn't realise that, of course . . . .'

'Does it really matter?' asked Paddy.

'Not at all,' replied the Pebble, 'but there is just one thing to consider. At any moment a situation may arise that you want to escape from. If you leave me buried away down here you can see for yourself how long it takes to get hold of me—I bet you were all of half an hour coming along the corridor.'

'Oh I was,' Paddy agreed. He thought it had been quite a bit longer. 'Yes, I know you are perfectly right, and I ought to hide you much closer to the hut. Only—oh I do wish . . . .'

'Hi!' shouted the Pebble. 'Don't! Don't! You really *must* be careful!'

Paddy dropped it with a crash. 'What were you going to

wish for at that ridiculous moment?' asked the Pebble, glaring at him in the dark.

'Nothing! Only for some matches!' gasped Paddy, not daring to pick it up.

'Well for a clever boy you are really most extraordinarily stupid,' said the Pebble. 'I wouldn't trust myself in your hands for a moment! You had much better leave me here for the time being and trust to luck that things won't happen in my absence. Close up the hole above as best you can, and drag the slab across it. Then put back the three stones and sweep it all level. You might just be able to make it invisible.'

When he had pushed the Pebble into the smallest possible space he could find underneath the steps Paddy climbed to the top of the hole, whispered goodbye over the edge, and began the task of putting the stones back into place.

Halfway back along the passage he realised that the sky in the chink above his head was greyer than before and there were no more stars. It must be very, very early morning.

He stumbled through the crack into the cave, and across the shore to the hut, now just visible in the dawn. He climbed in through the window and dropped onto his bed. Sleep closed over him. He sank down, down, down into nothingness.

When he woke up Judy was playing his mouth organ, and the sun was high in the sky.

14
Judy

'Where were you last night?' Judy asked, breaking off in the middle of a tune.

'In bed,' said Paddy promptly.

'No you weren't! I woke up and you weren't here. And I woke up again and still you weren't here. And I woke up much later, just when it was beginning to get light, and you *still* weren't here!' said Judy. 'Where were you?'

'I went for a walk on the island,' said Paddy lamely.

'I don't believe you! I got out of bed and went out to see!' said Judy. 'I thought you might have gone fishing, but all your fishing things were here. I might have been *terrified* all alone,' she added reproachfully, after a pause.

'Sorry,' said Paddy shortly. 'Were you?'

'Well, no,' she admitted. 'I didn't think you'd go off and leave your whole precious island to *me*. But where were you?' she persisted.

'My great-grandmother always said: Ask no questions and you'll be told no lies!' said Paddy smugly.

Judy flared up at once. 'All right,' she said, 'I *won't* ask questions! But I know perfectly well where you were! You went into that cave and into that crack where you told me I couldn't go till Wednesday. Didn't you?'

Paddy said nothing.

'You went to hide something,' Judy accused him. 'To hide it from *me*! Oh you are *rotten*!'

She flung the mouth organ as far as she could hurl it across the sand.

'I wouldn't have come if I thought you wouldn't trust me,' she said, turning her back on him.

'You couldn't help it!' jeered Paddy. 'I wished for you

and you had to come whether you liked it or not!'

'Oh I hate you!' Judy cried, flinging sand at him. 'I thought we could have such a lovely time here together, but you have spoilt it already! I want to go home!'

'Go on then!' he jeered.

'I can't! I can't!' she stormed, kicking at the sand and beating it with her fists. 'I'd leave you this minute if I could. You brought me here. Paddy, do please send me home again! You know you can!'

Paddy looked at her with the tears streaming down her face, and knew that if the Pebble had been in his hand at that moment he would have wished her wherever she wanted to go, just to make her happy again. But that would have left him with no wishes at all, for the whole of the rest of his stay on the island. Not that anything could be worse than living with a cross, crying girl who blamed him for everything that went wrong.

'I guess I will go for a walk,' he said, getting up and strolling away down the shore.

Judy did not follow him, and when he returned half an hour later she was presiding, like a benevolent queen, over a beautiful breakfast laid out on the rocks.

'You must be hungry after all that walking,' she said kindly, and Paddy liked to think she was only speaking of his morning stroll.

'It all looks *good*,' he said. 'Judy, you are a wonder! Shall we end up with oranges?'

'Do you know, there are only five left,' she said ruefully. 'It's all my fault—I know it is! I ate some in the night, and some more this morning! I just can't seem to leave them alone. You can have three, and I'll have two. What shall we eat when they're all gone?'

'Berries,' said Paddy gloomily. 'They're nice at first, and then they get more and more boring. But never mind, let's eat the oranges while they're here. I won't leave you alone with them again.'

'We could have one each a day, and halve the last one,' Judy suggested, but they knew it would be torture to think of the lovely golden fruit waiting for them, and not to be able to touch it.

'I don't think I could ever get tired of oranges,' Judy said wistfully, turning the skin inside out and sucking it.

'If she had known, I bet my great-grandma would have sent us a *caseful*,' said Paddy. 'Don't you enjoy not having to wash up afterwards? I still do! Now I'm going fishing, and with luck we'll have fried fish for dinner. You can pick some of those flat grass blades. They taste just like chips!'

'I shall make a list of the stores,' Judy said, 'and we'll pile them up in the hut.'

Paddy fished, and presently helped to carry the stores from the cave into the hut. He halved the last orange with her to keep her happy.

There were too many stores to count or ration, but it looked as if there was enough food to last for a long while to come.

'That will save you from getting a bellyache like my great-gran did from eating berries,' Paddy said, but Judy groaned a little.

'I've got one already from eating oranges,' she said. 'I ate eleven! But it isn't a very bad one, and I'll sleep it off in the sun.'

She seemed to have forgotten about the cave and the secret Paddy would not tell, but early on the morning they called Wednesday Judy woke up with the cry: 'Today we are going to explore the cave!'

For once it was a dull and cloudy morning. The sea was grey. The palm trees drooped their fronds with no breeze to stir them. The sun sulked somewhere behind thick clouds

that hung like velvet curtains in the sky.

'It's a terrible day for exploring,' said Paddy.

'No it isn't,' Judy insisted, 'it's a good day! Because if it was sunny we'd want to be out of doors. But we can't waste any sunshine if we are in the cave.'

'Very well,' Paddy said resignedly, 'we'll go. You can lead and I'll follow. You won't like it! I've told you so and now you'll find out. Don't say I didn't warn you! *You* want to go—I don't! But I've told you I'll take you, so there you are! We'll need some matches. And we'll take a picnic lunch,' he added.

'Won't we be back by then?' asked Judy, startled, and then, 'Oh yes! Do let's take a picnic lunch!'

But they had hardly squeezed through the crack in the cave before large drops of rain began to fall. With the narrow passage open far above them to the sky, the rain trickled relentlessly on their necks, and splashed off the rocks on to their bare legs.

Judy put up with it for some time, and then she said: 'I think this place is awful! Where *does* it lead to, Paddy? Why can't you say?'

'I thought you wanted to explore,' he jeered, 'I told you you wouldn't like it when you got here. And now you know!'

'But I only want to see what's at the other end,' Judy grumbled. 'Why have you got to be so mysterious about it? If you only told me where it leads to I wouldn't have to go on asking. You *do* know, don't you?'

'Well,' he said reluctantly, 'it isn't anything much, not really. It's a round cave, rather like the one we came from, but that's all. Now are you satisfied?'

'No,' said Judy thoughtfully. 'There might be another crack in it, mightn't there? And there might be treausre lurking behind the crack.'

'There isn't!' said Paddy quickly.

'How do you know?'

'Because I've been there!'

'I bet you never looked properly!' Judy taunted him, 'I bet you just had a glance around and came away.'

'I didn't!' he said angrily. 'And anyway, I've been there three times, so there!'

'You *have*? Aha! So there *is* something worth going for!' cried Judy. 'Well, I'm going to find out for myself! You needn't come! I'll go alone!'

'It's miles and miles before you get there,' Paddy warned her, but Judy was scuttling ahead. 'Don't worry, I've got the lunch!' she called back to him.

It was horribly unpleasant in the wet passage. The rain was everything except cold. But it still made walking a misery.

Paddy could not bear the thought of Judy rooting in the cave by herself. He followed with the rain dripping on his back, cursing the moment he had ever thought of bringing a girl like this to his private island. Why couldn't she be decently timid and nervous? He had been terrified himself. But of course she knew he had been there and back before, and was around to look after her. He had forgotten the matches again, but he had also forgotten his club.

He caught her up quite quickly, and when at last they reached the cave it was just as Paddy had described it to her. Judy refused to be disappointed, but went round and round the rocky walls feeling for gaps and crannies that might offer secret places.

They ate their lunch sitting on the floor. Paddy was chagrined to find Judy had packed a box of matches with the food.

'Well of course,' she said brightly, 'we were going down a tunnel, weren't we? And probably to a cave. Of course we'd need matches!'

Because the cave was dry she was able to strike them, and again she wandered round the walls lighting up each corner as she reached it. 'I can't think why you made such a thing about just a cave,' she said crossly.

'*You* did! I didn't!' he snapped. 'I just like to have something private of my own, that's all!'

'Oh well then,' said Judy, 'let's go home!'

Crossing the cavern she tripped over the topmost of the three stones Paddy had put to hide the slab.

'Ow—ww!' said Judy, hopping about and holding her foot.

Paddy then made his big mistake. He rushed to the stone, put it back in place and began to cover it with sand.

'What are you doing that for?' Judy asked curiously, dropping her foot.

'Nothing!' he snapped, but she only stared at him.

'You *are* funny,' she said wonderingly. 'I can't make you out! I hurt my foot and you make a fuss of the stone! What's *wrong* with the stone?'

She was on all fours examining the stone she had kicked. Paddy had already picked up the picnic things and was halfway out of the cave.

'Come on,' he said impatiently. 'It's getting late!'

'Late!' she scoffed. 'There isn't a late! We don't have any time to live by! Look, Paddy, look! I can pick it up, and there's another one underneath it!'

'What about it?' he called back from the passage.

'Well, I can pick up that one too,' she said, and he heard stones being tossed across the cavern floor.

'Don't do that,' he shouted, but Judy took no notice.

'There's another one under that,' she called. 'Have you got the matches?'

He pretended not to hear. He was walking fast now, into

the dripping rain that fell from far above.

'I think the rain is stopping,' he called back, but there was no reply.

'She'll come. She'll have to come!' Paddy told himself. 'She's in the dark, or nearly. She won't dare stop there all alone....' But he knew that Judy, when her mind was made up, dared almost anything.

He thought he heard her exclaim something like: 'Got it!' and knew she must have arrived at the third stone, underneath which was the great slab. He had not been able to move it himself without a lever, and it was a comfort to think that Judy would not be able to either.

But he stopped and listened, and listened and listened, and when he heard nothing at all, and went on hearing nothing, he reluctantly turned back down the passage and peered into the cave.

There was no Judy. The dim light showed that every part of the cave was empty. But the three stones were scattered round the floor, and the big slab was exposed to view. It was pushed aside just wide enough to show a dull light coming up from below.

Judy had found the slab and pulled or pushed it aside and clambered down the steps into the chamber below.

And there she was going round and round the walls, just as she had searched the upper cavern, feeling, fumbling, striking matches, one after another—Judy did not seem to know the meaning of nerves.

'Look here, Paddy!' she was saying, just as if she knew he would come back to look for her. 'There's nothing at all, but it doesn't *feel* like nothing at all! I'm sure Mr Jonathan Pickering's treasure is somewhere in this cave, and I'm going to find out what it is.'

'But it's *his* treasure!' Paddy expostulated. 'He wouldn't want us to bust in and discover it!'

He was climbing down the stairs now, looking, always looking into the dark corner where the Pebble was. The light from the matches disguised any gleam, and Paddy breathed again.

'I think there must be a knob or a stone, or a *something* that will open up a whole treasure-house of gold and jewels!' Judy was saying. 'It's just a question of looking everywhere. I've only got three matches left. You look too! But you've been here before, haven't you?' she accused him, 'You *know* where the treasure is!'

'I haven't found any treasure, Judy, honest!' he told her sincerely. 'No jewels, no gold and silver! I've been down here, yes! But there's nothing at all like you are talking about. I absolutely swear there isn't!'

'I don't know how much to believe you,' Judy said reproachfully, 'but perhaps you are right! There goes our last match. Let's get out! We've got that horrid wet walk all the way home, and all for nothing. Go on! I'm coming. Up you go!'

Paddy went ahead. He had reached the last step and was just climbing out when he heard a cry from Judy.

'Paddy! Oh Paddy, I think I've found it!'

Paddy turned round and saw Judy plunging into the darkness behind the steps.

'I saw a gleam! I saw something shining and sparkling in the dark behind the stairs! Oh do come back and help me!'

But Paddy, turning round to look, and lying on his chest across the great slab, felt a downward sliding movement, underneath him. The slab was slipping, sliding, rolling into place.

He snatched his hand away just in time to prevent it being crushed between the rock and the steps, and the next minute the slab was fast in place.

Paddy was annoyed, not frightened, and he set to work

to move it away. After all, he had done it twice before, and Judy had done no more than push it. She had said so.

He shouted through the slab: 'Don't worry! I'll have you out in a minute!' But there came no answer. It was as if the stone fitted so exactly into place that not a sound penetrated inside or out. (But the Pebble's voice had penetrated?)

Judy was not a timid girl, but it must be an unnerving experience to be shut up in the dark down there, and at the end of her matches, unable to communicate with him at all.

He shouted till he was hoarse, and in between shouting he pushed and shoved the great stone slab, which seemed worse than obstinate. Everything was against him. Everything was building up to defy him. Even Judy. But Judy was being punished now.

For nearly an hour he called to her and battled with the slab, till his nails were broken and his hands bleeding. Then he tried to dig another entrance into the cavern, but in no time he came to solid rock, and remembered that the whole of the cavern ceiling had been made of stone.

If at that moment the Pebble had been in his hand he would have wished his last wish in getting Judy out of the cavern and safely back at his side. Never mind about the rest of the year, never mind about the end of the island—he couldn't let her down, he must rescue her and keep her safe whatever happened.

Once he got her out he would see to it that for ever after the Pebble was used only to good effect. Never mind about companionship—he would keep it safely in his private cave and see to it that Judy only wished the wishes that he put into her mouth.

He remembered that the second time he had gone into the cavern he had moved the slab with his club, and at last, very reluctantly, he made up his mind to go home and fetch it.

He shouted his intention into the silent slab before running back as fast as he could through the sand, being buffeted from wall to wall, and bruised and grazed as he ran into the rocks at every corner.

Although he was running the way seemed longer than ever, and he was so worried and anxious he hardly noticed that it had stopped raining and was lighter than it had been before. Suddenly a gleam of sunshine slashed the passage, and the wet rocks glistened. The air was warm and damp. He could not be far now from the entrance and the hut.

He was trying to think where he had put his precious club? Was it in the bedroom, or down on the rocks?

He felt desperately guilty at having had to abandon Judy down there in the dark alone. His head was filled with growing terrors—her cries that never reached him, her battering on the roof, bruising her fists on the slab. She must be thinking him the most heartless creature in the world, but she could not possibly think it had been anything but an accident.

He almost fell through the crack into the sunshine on the shore.

There was a splendid feast spread out on the rocks between the shore and the cave, and presiding over the feast was Judy.

15
Reunion with the Pebble

'Why have you been such a long time?' she asked him with her mouth full. 'I've just begun. It is ages since we had anything to eat. I did wait for you, but one can't wait for ever.'

Paddy could only open and shut his mouth while he looked for words to express his fury and amazement.

'Why didn't you tell me?' he said at last. 'How did you come? Why didn't you say? Which way did you get here?'

Judy's face took on an air of mystery, tinged with malice. 'Oh well, there are ways and means!' she said innocently.

'What do you mean?' he raged at her. 'I've been worrying about you for hours and hours, ever since the slab slid back. Did you find another way out?'

Again the hint of mischief crossed her face. She looked out to sea and sighed gently. 'Of course I did!' she said.

'But how? Where? Which way?' Paddy pleaded. 'Do tell me Judy, for goodness' sake! It's *my* island!'

Judy's face closed up. 'Oh it is, is it?' she said. 'Then there's nothing I can tell you about it, is there?'

'Oh Judy, how can you be such a beast?' raged Paddy. 'If you knew what I've been through! It has been just so ghastly I can't talk about it! I pulled and pulled and shoved at the stone, and I shouted to you, but you never answered. Didn't you hear me?'

She shook her head.

'I thought you had done it on purpose!' she said coldly.

'Oh did you?' said Paddy. 'I'll never speak to you again!'

He vented his rage on the carefully laid-out feast, kicking it in all directions. Sand covered everything. Judy protected her eyes from the flying dust. She shrieked at him in vain. Not until he was exhaused did Paddy stop spreading chaos. Finally he rushed into the hut and flung himself down on his bed.

Some while later Judy appeared with cool spring water in a large shell, and bandages torn from her dress.

'You are in an awful mess,' she said kindly. 'I've come to clean you up a bit! And here is some chocolate. Will you let me wash your poor legs?'

Paddy's rage had cooled. He let her gently clean his scratches and bruises, and even thanked her when she had done. He hoped she might tell him of her own accord how she had escaped, but she did not. When he began on the subject a firm little line came to her lips, and a frown appeared between her eyes. He could not make her out. He had told her he was sorry about spoiling the feast she had made for him, and they were good friends again but as the days went by Paddy knew there was a shadow between them. Judy acted as though she had an advantage over him, and she never mentioned the cave.

She mended their 'Sulking Tent' on the far side of the island, and sometimes one or the other of them spent a few days in it, but they were always glad to see each other again.

They played endless games. Sand games, water games, ball games, rock games, squash, French cricket, fishing competitions at which Judy grew better and better, and Paddy grew worse and worse.

Slowly they were getting tired of one another. The days went by and they got more and more bored.

Paddy thought longingly of the Pebble, fast in its corner under the slab. He was almost certain by now that Judy had not got it. Nothing she said or did hinted that she knew anything about it, and this was a comfort to him.

He longed above all things to have a sensible, friendly chat with the Pebble. So one day, when they had quarrelled worse than usual, and he had gone off to the Sulking Tent, he turned aside instead, and started down the long passage to the cavern. He found his club in the cave, and this time he took it with him.

He was nearly there when he heard Judy's footsteps flying after him. The next minute her arms were round his neck and her hot, panting breath was in his ear.

'Don't go there, Paddy, don't! I'm sorry I was so horrible, I really am! It wasn't serious, was it? But don't go into the cavern! Please don't try! You see, if you do you may never get out again! It's true! It's perfectly true!'

'How did you know I was coming here?' Paddy demanded.

'I went to find you in the Sulking Tent because I meant to say I was sorry I'd been a beast, but you weren't there, so I went to the cave and your club had gone,' said Judy. 'So I came as quickly as ever I could. Look, do believe me! Don't go down that hole again! The stone may move for you, I daresay it will, but if it closes again you'll never get out without the Pebble . . . .'

'Without the *what*?' said Paddy, scandalised. After a moment he added hastily: 'But the Pebble is in there. I'm going to find it!'

'It isn't there,' Judy protested. 'It got me out the other day, I don't know how, but when I found it I was wishing I was out and so I was! I still had it in my hand. It isn't in the cavern any more, and without it you would just be shut in forever and die, I know you would! Let's leave the cavern alone, Paddy, and go back quickly and plan what we shall do next. We might almost ask the Pebble!'

Too ashamed to argue Paddy turned in his tracks and they went back together to the shore. This time Judy made no mystery about showing him where the Pebble was hidden—high in the rocks above the spring. The gleam of

the tumbling water disguised its shining eye.

'Did you know I had already used it?' Paddy asked when he held it again.

'Well, I worked it out that you must have,' Judy said, 'and that's how I arrived, and that's how you got your great-gran, Mrs Daisy Bucket! But I was frightened to try again, and that's why I hid it. I thought you might wish me away when we quarrelled. And I reckoned you were scared too, or you wouldn't have hidden it away down there in the dark. Do be careful of it!'

'Of course I will,' Paddy said, gently fondling the stone, 'Oh Pebble, I have missed you so!'

'I am glad to hear it!' said the Pebble.

Judy nearly fell over in her surprise.

'It *talks*!' she said, terrified.

'Of course it does! It is alive!' said Paddy calmly. 'Dear, dear old Pebble! My Pebble. My very own!'

'I am Jonathan Pickering's Pebble,' said the Pebble stiffly.

'Yes, yes, I know!' Paddy said hastily.

'And mine! I found it in the cavern!' said Judy jealously.

'You do realise,' the Pebble said, 'that Paddy now has only one wish left, and Judy has two? Anything may happen between now and the end of the year! When Judy was alone in the cavern I had to get her attention by all the means in my power. If she had not found me she might be there still!'

Paddy and Judy shuddered.

'Of course she wished to get out,' the Pebble said contemptuously, 'but she had to say it at the moment she was holding me in her hand. And if either of you should happen to wish a wrong wish, then you will be left with the result till the end of your tenancy of the island.'

'Pebble, you know Mr Jonathan Pickering told me there

must never be more than two people on the island at once?' Paddy said. 'Can you tell us what would happen if more people arrived?'

The Pebble shook itself slightly. 'I think—I *think* . . . ' it said solemnly, 'that if a lot of people came at once—things might—well, *anything* could happen!'

'What sort of things?' they both asked at once.

'Just anything . . . ' said the Pebble severely. 'Just anything not at all nice.'

They dared not ask any more, but Paddy lingered for one final word. 'Pebble,' he said, 'when I first came here I was absolutely happy. Why aren't I absolutely happy now?'

'You must have been wishing the wrong wishes,' the Pebble said severely. 'There is no reason at all why you should not be absolutely happy for a year on a beautiful island like this one. And you can't blame me! It is entirely your own fault!'

Paddy felt crushed and humiliated. He kicked a few stones out of his way before catching up with Judy, who was clutching the Pebble in her fist, as if she was afraid he would take it from her.

'I don't trust you with it,' she teased him. 'You could easily wish for the wrong thing! Just look at the way you have gone on till now!' Tenderly she unwrapped the Pebble from her handkerchief and caressed it.

'Dear Pebble! Good, kind Pebble! We simply can't trust him not to be foolish, can we, Pebble dear?'

'You sound just like my aunts!' Paddy jeered. 'Aunty Vi talks like that, and so does the squeaker aunty! They're both nutty!'

'I just wish your aunts could hear you!' Judy taunted him. 'They wouldn't be quite so sweet and loving about their dear little nephew who's gone to stay with great-grandma! They might even wish he'd stay away longer!

They . . . .'

But the icy chill that had fallen upon Paddy struck her so violently that she dropped the Pebble into the waterfall. Before stooping to pick it up she followed his petrified gaze towards the shore, where, tending a small camp fire, built with Girl Guide precision, the two aunts were busying themselves with preparing dinner. Paddy only looked at them for a few seconds before turning on Judy with white-faced fury.

'Now who is a fool?' he demanded.

16
The Aunts

'They haven't seen us yet,' Judy stammered. 'Don't take any notice! Find the Pebble again, quick, and wish them away!'

But it was daylight, and the sparkling, tumbling spring hid the twinkle of the Pebble's eye. The splashing and bubbling of the water drowned Paddy's calls to it. Knee-deep in the spray they frantically searched and fumbled.

'I'm terribly sorry,' Judy kept repeating. 'I didn't mean *that*—you know I didn't!'

'I don't care what you meant! You said it!' Paddy muttered angrily. 'You've lost your last-but-one wish, and now we only have one each to last us till we go home. And that's not the worst of it! Now we are four people on the island, not just two, and as the Pebble said—anything may happen!'

'Just anything,' Judy repeated blankly.

'But it couldn't be worse than the aunts,' said Paddy, and even as he said it he realised that a quite unlooked for and homesick part of him was glad to see them, a thought that he crushed as quickly as it came.

'Children!'

The cry came winging across the shore.

It was such a long time since he had been addressed in that way that Paddy merely stared.

'Children!' came the cry again. 'Dinner's ready!'

'We'd better go,' Judy said, but Paddy was anxious to find the Pebble, and bent over the water as if he had not heard the summons.

'You go. I'll follow,' he murmured, and reluctantly Judy started down the bank without him.

'Paddy!' the aunts shouted a few minutes later. 'Come along! It's all ready now!'

Aunty Jay had her arm round Judy's shoulders.

'Paddy!' they were all shouting.

Long habit made him obey.

'What were you looking for, dear?' One would have thought they had parted at breakfast time.

'Just a stone,' he said shortly.

Aunty Jay was quite pretty, he noticed. He had never thought of it before. He almost hoped she might kiss him after so long an absence, but she did not seem to think of it.

'Isn't it nice to have Judy with us?' Aunty Vi said. 'And such a lovely dinner! Yummy yummy!'

The stew was the Girl Guide stew she made at home, and it was indescribably delicious. If Paddy had not been so worried he would have thought of nothing else, but several problems were whirling round inside his head, and he could not give all his attention to something even as tasty as the food.

How long did the aunts intend to stay?

Where were they going to sleep if they did?

What was going to happen to the island now there were more than two people on it?

And where, oh where was the Pebble?

Once found, how important it would be to hide it again, since it seemed that by Pickering's law the aunts would be eligible too for three wishes each, and could become so powerful that he and Judy might as well pack up and leave them to it.

'Will you children do the washing-up?' Aunty Vi said when the food was finished. 'Aunty Jay and I are going to have a game of squash.'

'There's no ball,' said Paddy.

'We brought one,' said Aunty Vi, triumphantly fishing a

squash ball out of her pocket.

'Can we have a game after you?' Judy asked.

'When you have washed and tidied up,' the aunts chorused cheerfully, moving away towards the hut.

Paddy and Judy looked at each other and grinned.

'Did you hear them? No question of who is boss here!' said Paddy in disgust. 'They ought to know they are only here by invitation. By *your* invitation!' he added, rounding crossly on Judy, 'So you can wash up!'

'There isn't any washing-up,' she protested. 'Only the stewpan—ugh! We can throw the leaves away. The aunts have their little Girl Guide spoons and forks, but we don't need to wash our sticks, do we? Let's just wipe out the pan and leave it to dry while we have a chat with the Pebble.'

'We haven't got the Pebble,' said Paddy. 'We simply must find it. I don't like the feel of things at all. For one thing, where are the aunts going to sleep at night? We can't all go in the hut, and I'm not turning out for them!'

But the aunts had brought a little tent. When their game of squash was over Paddy and Judy could see them putting it up under the trees.

Their own search for the Pebble had been quite in vain, and they decided to have a game before they looked again.

'You haven't washed the stewpan! You have only wiped it!' one aunt complained, tapping in tent pegs. 'Suppose you take it to the stream and fetch us some drinking water at the same time.'

'We have some terrible storms on this island,' Paddy said as if she had not spoken. 'What are you going to do if it rains?'

'Slacken the guy ropes!' Aunty Vi said in triumph. 'And be very careful not to rub against the canvas! Though the flysheet should keep us safe and dry . . . .'

'Get the water, dear!' Aunty Jay said impatiently. 'I'm

terribly thirsty after our game, and that dish is really disgusting! Look at the flies! Take it away, Paddy, and wash it properly this time!'

Paddy picked up the stewpan, but stopped uncertainly, looking at his aunts. He wanted to borrow the squash ball, but he did not want to submit to their bossing any more.

Judy came to his rescue. 'I suppose you know . . . ' she said with a superior air, 'that this island belongs to Paddy?'

The aunts stared at her.

'What do you mean?' Aunty Vi asked.

'He has rented it for a year,' Judy went on. 'He has rented it from Mr Jonathan Pickering. You can ask the estate agent if you don't believe me. You know the office—just round the corner from Paddy's home. Paddy signed a contract, I believe. Didn't you, Paddy?'

'Yes,' he said flatly. 'Yes, I did!'

'But how much did you pay for it?' both aunts burst out together. 'Paddy hasn't that amount of money!' they added accusingly to Judy. 'Rented property is very expensive—especially islands!'

Judy laughed, but Paddy did not. He wanted to stop Judy at that point, but she went on boldly: 'As a matter of fact, he hasn't paid the rent yet! He'll pay at the end of the year.'

The aunts immediately relaxed. They smiled and nodded and made understanding noises.

'Well in that case it is hardly Paddy's island yet, is it?' they remarked. 'Do take away those horrid flies and fetch us some nice clean water.'

Without the Pebble Paddy felt helpless. More to get away from them than to obey orders he wandered off with the stewpan and a cloud of happy flies that buzzed about his head, as if he, and not the pan were in need of washing.

Judy to his disgust took on Aunty Jay at squash and beat

her hollow. That at least gave her some advantage over the invading aunts. He did not offer to play them himself. If one of them beat him (as Judy often did) well . . . .

It became very important to find the Pebble.

When he returned with the water the two aunts and Judy were making lists of the stores in the cave. Paddy was almost too angry to speak.

'But they are *my* stores!' he spluttered at last.

'Yes dear, but we must know how much food we have got to last us,' said Aunty Vi soothingly. 'We aren't eating it, we are only writing it down. Judy, I've counted thirty-five tins of fruit—have you missed any? And what about cereals? Have you started on those? And dried milk . . . .'

'But they're *mine*!' Paddy said passionately. 'My great-grandmother sent them to me. They're not for listing and giving out like rations! They're to eat when we want them!'

'Yes, dear,' said Aunty Jay, patiently writing.

'It's quite a good idea really, Paddy,' said Judy, deep in packages. 'Because now we are four we shall use them up much more quickly. We really need to know how many supplies we have got.'

'But how long are you going to stay?' Paddy demanded, putting down the water jug so violently that the water slopped on the floor. 'It's for *me* to give out the food, not Judy! And not you either! I can send you away whenever I want to!' he shouted angrily. 'I never asked you to come here! It was Judy who did! And it was all a mistake,' he added. 'It was just her silly fault when she told me about my having stupid wishes and then she goes and does it herself! I tell you it is *my* island and none of you has any business here at all! I just wish you would GO AWAY! Go on! GO!' he shouted, but the aunts and Judy just stared at him, and he realised that without the Pebble he was powerless to make them do anything at all.

Dashing out of the cave he climbed the bank to the spring, and began to search frantically for the only hope he had of getting his powers back.

Once he found the Pebble he was fully determined to send the three of them packing: Judy, Aunty Vi and Aunty Jay. They could go back to where they came from, and good riddance to the lot of them!

But he did not find the Pebble, and when darkness fell nothing gleamed at him out of the tumbling water.

The aunts and Judy had built a little fire, and were singing camp fire songs outside the tent. It smelt as if they were drinking cocoa. It all looked very friendly and tempting and comfortable, and he would have liked to join them, but his pride would not allow it.

He went up to the hut by a wide detour, removed his bedding and his clothes and all his transportable possessions, and dragged them to the Sulking Tent on the other side of the island.

17
The Guides

Paddy did not sleep very well. He worried incessantly about the lost Pebble. He could not believe that he would never see it again, but by now he knew that the water rushed down over the rocks driving little sticks and stones before it, and after quite a long course it tumbled on to the shore and made its way to the sea.

In the middle of the night he left the Sulking Tent and followed the stream back across the shore and up the rocks to the spring at the top of the fall, but never a glimpse of the shining eye did he see.

Instead, he found Judy waiting for him on the sands, and it was like a long-lost friend to see her alone without the aunts.

'You didn't tell them, did you?' he asked her anxiously, for that had been his second worry. Once the aunts knew that they had the right to three wishes each from the Pebble, they would hardly sleep till it was found, and the powers it would give them were terrible to imagine.

'No, of course, I didn't!' she scoffed. 'But it was silly to go off to the Sulking Tent by yourself. They're quite nice old things, you know! Not really bossy—in fact . . . .'

'Children!' came a call from the little tent. 'What are you doing out there at this time of night? You should both be in your beds.'

'And did you *wash*?' came a second voice.

'There you see!' said Paddy. 'Do you call that not being bossy? I'm not going near them till I find the Pebble. You can do as you like, it's all the same to me, but don't whatever you do tell them the whole story or we'll be lost! It's bad enough not knowing what is going to happen next, if what the Pebble said is true. It's bound to be something nasty. I just must get the Pebble back so that at least we can escape if we want to.'

'And leave your aunts here?' said Judy doubtfully.

'Well.'

'I suppose it's their own fault . . . ' she said resignedly.

'No it isn't! It's yours!' snapped Paddy. 'They didn't choose to come here! You wished it for them. And if we get away and they don't it will still be your fault. Anything could happen to them, all through you!'

'Oh Paddy, I didn't mean it,' said Judy, nearly in tears. 'You know it was all a mistake. I really don't want anything horrid to happen to them if we can help it.'

'Well, nothing has happened yet,' said Paddy staunchly, 'but if it does, we haven't even got the Pebble to stop it with. I don't know what we are going to do. I'm going to have just one more proper hunt, and then . . . .'

'Children! *Will you* go to bed!' came Aunty Vi's voice from the tent. 'It's half past three, and you ought not to be running about on the shore at this time of night. Go back to the hut at once!'

Paddy shrugged his shoulders.

'You go back,' he said, 'I'll wait till they settle, and then I'll try searching again. Goodnight, Judy!'

Half an hour later he crept into the Sulking Tent with no Pebble, no hope of success, and no expectation of sleep.

Yet he had not curled up for more than three minutes before the world around him faded out, and he began to snore.

In the morning the aunts were like two schoolgirls. They ran about the shore in bare feet with their skirts kirtled up round their waists. Their laughter annoyed Paddy very much. Two adult peals and one child's. He could not think what Judy could find to be funny about in the company of the aunts.

Then there was a kind of silence, and looking round he saw they were all quartering the shore and searching, searching . . . .

Somehow he did not like the look of that either. He wandered across the sands and crossed Judy's track.

'What's it all about?' he asked carelessly. 'Can't you take them over to the other bay?'

'Oh no,' she said seriously, 'we're looking for shells. Very special shells that open in the middle like butterflies and you see, it gives *me* a chance to look for the Pebble!'

Paddy saw the sense of this and joined in the search. So he was there when, a little while later, Aunty Vi held up her hand and exclaimed: 'Now I've got a *very* funny one!'

They joined her, and saw, lying in her palm the unmistakable presence of the Pebble, complete with its wide and shining eye. Paddy could have sworn that it was winking at him.

When Judy saw it she caught her breath, but she had the good sense not to shout aloud or to betray her feelings. She just tensed all over like a spaniel when it scents a bird, and Paddy, who was standing next to her, felt her trembling.

'Shut up!' he murmured to her.

'That's pretty,' he said to Aunty Vi. 'Please can I have a look at it?'

Paddy's voice was so polite, so different from the gruff way he had previously addressed his aunts, that they noticed it at once. Aunty Vi's fist closed quickly over the Pebble.

'Have you seen one here before, dear?' she asked, scrutinising the stone between her fingers. 'I think it looks so interesting!'

Paddy's immediate answer was to snatch at the Pebble in her hands. ('Oh you fool! You fool!' moaned Judy.)

Aunty Vi at once held it high above her head.

'You are a very rude little boy! I wish you would keep your hands to yourself,' she said crossly. 'Of course you shall have a look at it, but you might at least ask politely. Look, I'll put it on this rock, and then we can all see it. Do you see how the bit in the middle shines? It is very like an eye, I think.'

Paddy discovered to his fury that he could no longer reach for the Pebble. Some invisible force held his hands to his sides the moment he came within a metre of it.

He gazed in agony at Judy, but Aunty Jay was holding her tightly, as if afraid she might make a grab for it as Paddy had done, and Judy was watching it intently, refusing to catch Paddy's eye.

'I think,' said Aunty Vi, picking it up again, 'that I shall put it among my favourite treasures and souvenirs of this island. I'll keep it till I get home in the little case I hang round my neck—there I know it will be perfectly safe. That's all that matters for the moment.' She pulled out the locket on the end of a long chain that hung low inside her blouse, and the next minute the Pebble was lost to view.

Paddy tried to call to it, but no reply came, and the aunts looked at him as if he were mad.

'Never mind,' said Judy, joining him later in the Sulking Tent. 'We both know where it is now, and we know it is safe. That's all that matters at the moment. Let's go for a walk and forget about it.'

Paddy and Judy went for a walk by themselves, while the aunts dozed in the sun. They felt partly reassured, because nothing terrible had happened on the island since the arrival of the aunts. The weather was beautiful. There was plenty of food. They had found the Pebble, and sooner or later they would get it back again.

But when, much later, they returned, the sun was going down, and there was a whole company of Girl Guides encamped below the hut, where the aunts' tent was pitched.

Paddy turned to Judy, expecting to see the same disgust on her face as on his own, but Judy was radiant.

'Oh what *fun*,' she exclaimed, and set off across the sand shouting for pleasure.

Paddy remembered that Judy had just joined the Guides, and the idea of a Guide camp on the island could only appeal to her very strongly. She did not stop to consider that the island, bound by Pickering's law to hold only two inhabitants, was now overrun by two aunts and at least twenty Girl Guides between the ages of ten and sixteen. What this meant in terms of overcrowding was beyond all imagination.

Paddy didn't trust Judy any more. He could see her now with the Guides, talking excitedly now to one and now to another. Sooner or later, surely, she would tell them about the stone, and the cave, and the long, winding passage that led to it. 'Girls are such blabbers!' thought Paddy. He longed to dash into their midst and wrest the Pebble from its prison in the locket hanging round Aunty Vi's neck. But he knew his hands were powerless to snatch or strike. Even as he planned it his fists felt numb. His hands fell by his sides.

'They shan't borrow my tent,' he muttered to comfort himself, but already camping tents were being pitched, the fire was being stoked with driftwood, pots were hung on tripods, and food fetched from the cave.

'*My* food!' thought Paddy angrily.

He waited till the sun sank, and the glow of the fire lit up a circle of happy faces. Once he thought he saw Judy point in his direction, so he turned his back on her and walked away.

Slowly he walked round the outskirts of the island, till he came back at last to his Sulking Tent.

Through the trees the glow of the fire was reflected, and the sound of songs and choruses woke a nostalgic echo in his heart.

He flung himself into his tent, and lay awake a long, long time.

18
Return of the Pirates

In the morning Judy bounced into his tent and woke him up.

'Oh Paddy, you don't mind it really, do you?' she pleaded. Her eyes were bright with excitement and she could hardly sit still. 'You can't think what fun it is to have the Guides here! We've planned a Great Stalking Game—half on one end of the island and half on the other. We have to try to get to each other's ends without being caught.'

'Tom Tiddler's Ground,' suggested Paddy sarcastically.

'Sort of—only not being seen,' said Judy.

'What about the aunts?'

'Oh they're each one end,' Judy explained. 'And I'm on one side and we hoped you might be on the other . . . .'

'Who's *we*?'

'The Guides and I,' said Judy. 'You see, it gives the other side an advantage if they don't have a person like me with them who knows the island, like you and I do . . . .'

'Then don't join them. Stay out of it like me,' Paddy said defiantly. Judy's face fell.

'Not so good,' she remarked. 'For one thing, they might find the passage out of the cave, and we don't want that, do we?'

'I don't see that it matters if the Pebble isn't there,' said Paddy wearily. 'It seems to me that instead of playing silly games we could be thinking how to get the Pebble back from Aunty Vi. Do you think she realises how she got her wretched Girl Guides here? Do you think either of the aunts has the slightest *idea*?'

Judy shook her head.

'No, I don't,' she said decidedly. 'For one thing, this

morning when Aunty Vi was washing her neck she took off her locket, and I distinctly heard her say: 'Oh I do wish I had my camera here to take some snaps of the girls!' But of course the camera didn't come because she wasn't holding the Pebble. It was hanging on a twig!'

She giggled wildly.

'Then why didn't you rush and take it?' cried Paddy in exasperation.

'Oh I couldn't,' said Judy, shocked. 'I wasn't as close to her as all that—and then, she had her undies hanging up too, and she wouldn't have liked it.'

'I know,' said Paddy. 'You *like* having your blasted Guides all over the place. You don't want them to go away. Well, let me tell you one thing. If I ever get the Pebble in my hands again I'll wish the whole lot of you back where you came from! And I'll have the whole island entirely to myself as it was before.'

He knew he had said the wrong thing, because Judy went quite white, and twisted her hands in and out of the blanket. Slowly her colour came back, and she got off the bed. But before she had left the tent two Girl Guides burst in upon them.

'Do you know there's a big ship out at sea!' they chorused. 'And we think it's heading this way! We waited to see what kind of a flag it is flying, and whatever do you think? It's a skull and crossbones!'

Paddy was out of bed in a minute. Some acute instinct told him to beware. It was all very well to remember that his great-grandmother might still be on board, and probably was, but he also remembered that a certain threat was due to fall on the island, and what was more likely than an invasion by pirates?

Else why, *why* were they coming back? Could they possibly have become aware of Jonathan Pickering's treasure—his wishing-stone? And were they coming to collect it and take it away?

At once Paddy's sense of ownership took charge, and he rushed to summon the Guides, who were staring on the seashore.

'Listen, everybody!' Paddy commanded, and every face turned towards him. 'I can tell you one thing! These are pirates coming! They've been here before, and they took away my great-grandmother to be their cook. Now they are coming back again, and whether they are coming as baddies or as goodies I just don't know. It depends on the sort of mood they are in. I think they just might be coming to look for Mr Jonathan Pickering's treasure, but in any case they had better not find all of you here!'

'Judy!' he called, and reluctantly she came back to him. 'I want you to take all these girls into the cave, and make them stay there until I tell you it is safe for them to come out. Take all the tents with you as you go. You are to take them along the secret passage and hide them in the cavern at the very end. You had better go last, I think!'

'How far is it?' asked Aunty Jay, shivering. 'And how dark? If Judy is this end, who is going to lead us?'

'I will,' said Aunty Vi calmly. 'I have been there before. Come along, girls!'

With the Girl Guides sobbing and snuffling, and carrying their possessions, she led the way across the sands to the cave, where one by one they disappeared through the entrance.

Judy was last. 'I'll stay with you,' she said bravely.

'No, you won't!' Paddy said firmly. 'You go after them and stop them from talking, or coming back if they are frightened of the dark. What luck that the sun is coming up! That means the passage won't be pitch dark either. Have you got a torch?'

'The battery is dead,' she said flatly.

'Oh well, that's that then! Goodbye!'

Paddy turned back towards the sea. With Judy gone the island felt utterly deserted.

He could see the masts of the pirate ship now, creeping slowly round the western point of the island, and he guessed the pirates could see him too. He strained his eyes to try to find the figure of his great-grandmother on the bridge, but there was no great-grandmother to be seen.

He was touched that Judy had wanted to stay with him, in spite of her rotten Guides and the aunts and all the fun she was having without him. She was a great girl in spite of her faults, and he did not want to see any harm come to her. Neither did he want to see the aunts harmed, nor the Girl Guides, some of whom were very pleasant indeed.

Well, if the pirates were really after the treasure he could say quite truthfully that he did not know where it was, because only Aunty Vi knew where she had hidden the Pebble.

Now Paddy could see figures on the deck, one standing silently on the bridge, but there was no sign anywhere of his great-grandmother.

When he raised his hand and waved not a single hand returned his greeting. The ship came on, but nobody hailed him or called, 'Ahoy!'

Rather closer to the beach than on the first occasion the pirate ship dropped anchor. It was so large it seemed to loom like a mountain on top of Paddy, but just as he was trying to invent a proper greeting for the return of his visitors, the pirates began to drop over the sides into various small boats below.

Boat after boat filled with pirates and rowed rapidly towards the shore. He looked in vain for the figure of Mrs Daisy Bucket. She was not there.

In the very last boat of all came the pirate captain. Suddenly Paddy became very, very frightened indeed. All kinds of possibilities came into his head to account for the grim and menacing return of the pirates to the island, without his great-grandmother.

Had her cooking been so appalling that they had already cast her away on a different island? But Mrs Daisy Bucket cooked the best dinners Paddy had ever eaten. Could she have tried to poison the pirates and if so, why?

The first of the boats landed on the beach and the rest followed. The pirates shipped their oars, left their boats, and formed a guard of honour for their captain, who stepped ashore, and strode up the sand to Paddy's side.

With his left hand he gave him such a clout that Paddy's head reeled. With his right hand the captain seized him by the shoulder and shook him to and fro like a rag.

'Where . . . ' roared the captain. 'Where, you miserable midget, is Jonathan Pickering's treasure?'

Breathless from the shaking Paddy staggered back a pace or two. It took all his courage to look the captain in the face, but look he did. 'What treasure?' he demanded bravely.

All the pirates broke into loud laughter.

'Quiet!' roared the captain. He went down on one knee till his face with its black moustaches and the silver rings in his ears were on a level with Paddy's nose.

'You thought you were a clever little lad,' snarled the pirate captain. 'You thought you could pull the wool over the eyes of the pirate captain and his crew! You sent us away with the old lady, your great-grandmother, and the old lady made us send you a whole cargo of delicious provisions when all the time you could get all the good things you ever wanted with Jonathan Pickering's wishing-stone! Isn't that the truth, my little man?'

'No! No! No!' shouted Paddy.

'Come now!' said the captain, suddenly becoming gentle and persuasive. 'You have got the stone, haven't you? Suppose you just let *me* have it, and we'll go away!'

'I haven't got it! I haven't!' Paddy insisted.

'Then perhaps you know where it is hidden?' the captain coaxed '"Ask my great-grandson!" the old lady said! And that was just before she walked the plank!'

'*She walked the plank*?' Paddy gasped. 'You made my great-grandmother walk the plank?'

The pirates looked sheepish. The captain fixed his gaze on a distant rock and rose to his feet.

'So now you know,' he said softly. 'Most unpleasant things happen to people who don't tell the truth to the pirate captain. "What do you know about Jonathan Pickering's treasure?" we asked the old lady. "Nothing," she said, "There is no treasure!" But we went on asking, even when she was so seasick that her cooking got worse and worse. Presently, when she had given us tapioca for a week we threatened her with the plank if she did not tell us all she knew. "Ask my grandson!" she said, and the next moment you could see she wished she had bitten her tongue off. So—we—er—so . . . .' He stopped, and all the pirates looked the other way.

Paddy stared open-mouthed at the tyrant standing before him. This brute, this demon, this master-villain had dared to dispose of his beloved, generous, loving great-grandmother, and in a manner that he could hardly bear to imagine.

To think of Mrs Daisy Bucket walking off the end of a plank into the sea was a scene that smashed his world into small fragments. Her kind, round, pink face; her stores; her funny sayings; her kind and loving heart—all gone, all vanished underneath the waves, to suit a pirate's greedy whim. It was too hard to bear, and suddenly Paddy turned on the captain like a firebrand and attacked him with his fists and with his feet, kicking, biting, screaming with fury and indignation.

'You dared! You dared lay hands on my great-grand-mother!' he yelled. 'You made her walk the plank into the sea! You drowned here! I hate you! I hate you! I HATE YOU!'

The captain shook him off like a snapping puppy. At the same time the crew closed in and seized him, one man holding him by the legs and the others by the arms. A fourth put a big hand over his face and held his jaw fast.

'Put him in the boat!' the captain commanded. 'Take him back to the ship. And the rest of you—search every nook and cranny on the island for Jonathan Pickering's treasure! Don't give up till you find it! You can signal me from the point when you do! I'll go back with the boy, and two of you men can row us. Tie him up with your belt, Matt, or the young rascal may try to escape. We'll ask him some more questions once we get him on board.'

Some little while later Paddy, with his hands tied behind his back, was standing on the deck in front of the pirate captain, refusing to say a single word.

He kept up his courage by thinking of Judy in the cave, safeguarding the aunts and the frightened Girl Guides. But if the pirates found them—what then? Only Judy knew that the stone had powers. To the others it was just a curiosity. And if the pirates found out that Judy knew, would they—could they—make *her* walk the plank too? Paddy began to feel sick with fear.

'Put him in the hold!' the pirate captain ordered, when nothing would persuade him to speak, and down the ladder into the darker depths of the hold went Paddy.

The hatch clanged to over his head.

19
In the Hold

'Come here, dear, and let me unfasten your hands,' said a voice from the corner of the hold.

There, sitting upright and dignified was his great-grandmother, Mrs Daisy Bucket.

Paddy stumbled across to her in the darkness, found her enveloping arms and burst into tears.

'I thought they made you walk the plank!' he said when she had unfastened his wrists and rubbed the red welts made by the belt that bound them.

'Oh they did!' his great-grandmother agreed. 'But not into the sea. I explained to them that I couldn't swim. So I walked the plank down into here. It was quite bad enough.'

'You might have broken your leg!' sniffed Paddy. 'It was terribly cruel.'

'Not at all! Not at all!' soothed Mrs Bucket. 'You must have noticed there is straw all over the floor. Very dirty straw,' she added with a sniff. 'Very smelly, dirty straw, but quite soft. I did twist my ankle a little bit, but nothing was broken, thank goodness. And I brought it on myself of course! I ought never, never to have mentioned my great-grandson. I am so very sorry to have brought you into this trouble, Patrick dear!'

'It's quite all right,' he assured her. 'It was terrible when I thought you were drowned. I couldn't bear it! But what is going to happen if they get into the cave and the passage and find all the Girl Guides and Judy and the aunts?'

'The *what*? The *who*? The *which*?' exclaimed Mrs Daisy Bucket, in horror.

Paddy related what had happened since she went away to be a ship's cook.

'Oh my goodness!' said his great-grandmother. 'It never rains but it pours! I did wonder how you were getting on there all by yourself, but I never thought you would bring along the aunties! Poor Vi! Poor Jay! Whatever do they make of it all?'

'I didn't bring them along—Judy did!' Paddy said indignantly. 'She said she wished my aunts could see me now, and of course they did. I was horrified, Great-Grandma, just horrified! And they like it, the aunts do! They're camping out just as they used to do at home. Judy likes it too. It wasn't so bad when I just had her for company.'

'I suppose *you* wished for her?' his great-grandmother sugggested.

'Well, yes I did,' Paddy admitted. 'It got kind of lonely when you were gone. We had good times, didn't we?'

'We did indeed?' said Mrs Daisy Bucket. 'I was quite sorry to leave you. And I hope you enjoyed all those provisions I made the pirates send you?'

'They were terrific!' Paddy said. 'There was enough for the aunts and the Guides and all of us. Enough to last a year at least! Don't they give you anything to eat down here, Great-Grandma?'

'Oh yes, plenty!' his great-grandmother said wrily. 'I have a whole pail of tapioca in the corner!'

He could almost hear her grimacing in the dark.

'How awful!' Paddy said. He wondered how long he would have to stay in the hold before he could face eating tapioca.

'It isn't bad really,' she reassured him, 'not unless you are feeling seasick. But don't let's think about it till we are really hungry. Shall I tell you a story?'

The hours passed quickly under the magic of his great-grandmother's tongue. Long before dawn they were both sleeping soundly.

20
Rescue by Judy

In the morning the hatch was suddenly raised and sunshine poured down into the hold.

If Paddy had expected to see the pirate captain or one of the crew, he was infinitely surprised to see Judy.

'Come along! Come along quickly!' she told them. 'They're all asleep—even the Guides! Everybody has been stuffing themselves silly with the provisions. We bunged up the crack with bags and boxes, and inside the passage we passed them like bucket drill along to the cavern. It kept the girls from crying. And the pirates helped themselves from the outside. They had no idea we were hiding down there! We could hear them grumbling about the frightful food they'd had to eat on board. Your great-grandmother's cooking, of course!'

'My great-grandmother is the best cook in the world!' said Paddy proudly. 'And here she is, anyway!'

Judy remained confused for a mere half second. 'Did you cook that awful great pail of milk-pudding?' she asked. 'No wonder they all hated it! Come and have something nice with us in the cave. I've pinched one of their boats, and we'll row round the back of the island and land on the north shore. Come on! The ladder is quite easy. You push her, Paddy, and I'll pull. Up she comes! Now down another ladder, Mrs Bucket, and you'll be there. Take my hand.'

'But how did you get *out*?' Paddy asked her, when all three were safely in the rowing boat and pulling away in the shadow of the pirate ship.

'Ssh! Voices carry over the water,' Judy warned him. 'I just waited till they left the cave, and then I picked my way out through the bags like a mouse and stuffed them up again. The pirates were up at the hut, and I think they've all gone to sleep, they were so tired looking for the treasure.'

'Who has got it?' whispered Paddy.

'I don't really know. I think Aunty Vi put it in the final cavern, but she may have forgotten by now. I want you to come and find it. You see, if any of the Guides find out what it really is we could be in the most terrible danger. Any of them might wish something quite disastrous before we could stop them,' Judy said. 'You know yourself how easy it is to make something happen that you don't want at all. And there are twenty Guides as well as the aunts and Great-Gran and you and me, and we've used up all but two of our own wishes. It's better for all of us to be together before we even begin to wish, and that's why I came for you, Paddy.'

'Thank you,' he said coolly. How quickly Judy took things in hand and became bossy!

They were beyond the point of the island by now, and invisible from the main shore. Judy and Paddy each manned an oar. Quite soon they landed the boat in a little creek, and climbed into the undergrowth, with Mrs Daisy Bucket limping between them.

'I'll go ahead now, and see how the land lies,' Paddy said, taking up his position as leader. 'You two stay here in the bushes till I come.'

'Oh well, if that's the way you want it,' said Judy, aggrieved. She liked to think of herself as the rescue party, and here was Paddy asserting his authority as if she hardly counted. She crouched in the shrubs with Mrs Daisy Bucket and watched him out of sight.

When he had been gone a very long time she persuaded the old lady to climb up the hill, from which position they could look down on the south shore some distance away, but no Paddy and no pirates could be seen.

Paddy was, in fact, lying flat on his stomach outside

the house, and listening with all his ears to the pirate conference going on within. He knew he was in the most dangerous position on the island, and discovery might come at any time.

'One more search,' he heard the voice of the pirate captain pronounce, 'and if there is still no sign of the treasure we will set fire to the whole island and leave it.'

Paddy's blood ran cold.

What about Judy? What about his great-grandmother? And what about the aunts and the Girl Guides shut up inside the cavern? How could he possibly warn them and what was likely to happen to them if he did?

He lay fretting and listening as pirate after pirate described the caves he had searched, the corners he had explored and the holes he had excavated. It seemed they were all looking for a chest, since it was difficult to imagine treasure hidden in any other way. Paddy's imagination swelled to the picture of nineteen or so pirates each wishing for three times the amount of gold and jewels they could think of. Enough to sink the pirate ship!

Judy and Mrs Daisy Bucket waited in vain.

'I think they must have caught him,' Judy said miserably. 'He would never have left us so long without news. Shall we go back to the boat?'

But Mrs Daisy Bucket was exploring in the undergrowth and picking a few berries. 'Quite like old times,' she remarked, 'and I think the bees like them too! Can you hear them humming?'

Judy listened. She heard, not the buzzing of honey-loving bees, but the unmistakable hum of human voices in the earth way below their feet. Under the roots and the plants and the branches a deep fissure of rock ran across the jungle, and far down inside it people were talking.

'It's the Guides!' said Judy in excitement.

Mrs Daisy Bucket only stared.

'They're in the passage,' Judy explained. 'The pirates haven't found them, and the aunts are looking after them. We'd be much safer down there with them if Paddy doesn't come back soon. Are you game to try this way?'

Mrs Daisy Bucket squinted down into the crack. 'It doesn't look much more dangerous than the hold,' she pronounced. 'Just let me hitch up my skirts and I'll manage.'

'You go first, and I'll wait a bit longer for Paddy,' Judy said. 'You can ask Aunty Vi for the wishing-stone, and if she knows where she has put it you must ask her to let you hold it, and then you say—I'm not sure what you do say . . . ' she finished helplessly.

'And if she hasn't got it?' suggested Mrs Daisy Bucket.

'Well you *look* for it!' said Judy in exasperation. 'And when you do find it please, please bring it to me! I've only got one wish left, but I'll think of something to get us all out of this mess! The only thing I want to do is to stay here with Paddy, but we don't really need the aunts, nor the Guides, I suppose,' she ended regretfully. 'And above all we don't want the pirates! Perhaps we can just get rid of the pirates! But that leaves the aunts and the Guides, and it makes Paddy cross. And it does seem to bring bad luck too. I mean, I'm sure it was having all those people here that brought the pirates . . . .'

'We have to find the Pebble first,' Mrs Daisy Bucket gently reminded her. 'Why don't you come down with me?'

'I'd like to,' Judy said, 'but how would I tell Paddy I had gone? And how would I ever get back again? We aren't even absolutely sure that the Pebble wishing-stone is down there, are we?'

The last thing she saw of Mrs Daisy Bucket was an

avalanche of earth, as the old lady hitched up her skirts and slid over the edge of the crack into the ravine.

'Keep quiet!' Aunty Vi urged the startled Guides. 'Come along after me on tiptoe, all of you! Are you all right, Gran dear? Can you lean on me? And the rest come after! Don't say a word till I tell you to!'

The little party wound its way to the far end of the passage. Once inside the cavern Aunty Vi made them all sit in a ring before she allowed them to talk, and before any other explanations she wanted to know where Judy and Paddy were, and why they had not come with Great-Grandmother Bucket, who had arrived in such an unceremonious way.

'Judy is coming in a minute,' Mrs Daisy Bucket explained. 'She has gone to look for Paddy, and Paddy has gone to look for the pirates. They are searching for Jonathan Pickering's treasure.'

'If the pirates find Jonathan Pickering's treasure they may go away and leave us in peace,' said the Guides. 'Do you think one of our patrols could go back to the entrance and get us some more choc bars and some ginger beer? We haven't got anything left to eat and we are all so hungry!'

'It's not safe, not while they are hunting,' said Mrs Daisy Bucket. 'And however hard they look they won't be able to find the treasure—it isn't there! It is much closer to us than that. In fact, I think it is quite possible that one of you may be sitting on it!'

The Guides leapt up with shrieks of excitement, and every expectation of finding a treasure chest buried in the sand. In the dim light of the cavern they delved and dug and worried at the rocky corners, and even at the bricks in the centre of the ring, but nothing revealed itself.

Mrs Daisy Bucket continued to sit complacently in the

ring looking at her boots.

Aunty Jay and Aunty Vi made little dashes and darts entreating the girls to keep their voices low for fear of the pirates. They were not at all happy at the idea of having Jonathan Pickering's treasure practically on top of them, so to speak. Suppose the pirates got wind of it, and came after them through the original crack in the rock, or fell in from the top as Mrs Daisy Bucket had done?

They turned pleadingly to Paddy's great-grandmother and begged her to tell them all she knew. Mrs Daisy Bucket was comforted that neither of them had the least idea of the Pebble's powers.

'Have you still got that little—lucky stone that you picked up on the shore, dear?' she asked carelessly.

'Oh yes, I hope I have,' said Aunty Vi. 'It was a dear little stone, and I didn't want to lose it. I brought it along here yesterday, all by myself, when I first explored the passage. It reminded me of potholing in the Derbyshire caves. I meant to hide it in this very cavern till I took it home to England. It is so easy to lose things on an island, isn't it?'

'So very easy,' Mrs Daisy Bucket agreed. She felt like hugging dear Aunty Vi who was making it all so simple.

But at that moment there was a shout from the Guides, another bump and flurry of earth, and Judy, covered from head to foot with dirt, ran into the cavern quite breathless with haste and announced: 'I don't know where Paddy is, and I haven't seen him, but the pirates are coming out of the hut and swarming all over the island. We have got to be frightfully quiet and careful because if they find the place where Great-Gran slid into the ravine, or the one where I did, they'll know there is something going on down here, and they'll come down after the treasure!'

'It's all right, dear,' Mrs Daisy Bucket announced calmly. 'There is no need to be afraid! We are all perfectly safe, and Patrick too. Aunty Vi has got the treasure.'

'Aunty Vi!' exclaimed all the Guides and Aunty Jay.

'So if you will just let me hold the stone for one moment, dear,' said Mrs Daisy Bucket, 'I will get us all out of this painful situation in a second. The pirates have no idea quite how simple an object Mr Jonathan Pickering's treasure really is. They would be so astonished if they knew. Thank you, my dear, did you say you kept it in your locket?'

Aunty Vi had her hand at her neck where the locket hung, but her face was perfectly white.

'What did you say, Mrs Bucket? What did you mean?' she asked in a faint voice, and for a moment it looked as if she was going to refuse to give it up.

'I mean, dear, that Mr Jonathan Pickering's treasure is a wishing-stone!' said Mrs Daisy Bucket. 'And if you do not want me to have it you can perfectly well make a proper wish on it for yourself! Each of us has a right to three wishes!' she explained to the assembly. 'All you have to do is to repeat after me these few words. I wish . . . .'

Aunty Vi's mouth opened and closed once or twice like a goldfish. All the Guides were looking at her. Her face was flushed now, not pale.

'I think I have had my three wishes,' she whispered. 'Such strange things happened . . . .'

'What did you wish for?' snapped Judy. 'And when did you wish for them? I know you took away Paddy's power to take the stone from you. That was one stupid wish! What else?'

'Toilet paper,' murmured Aunty Vi. 'It was so awkward without, and there it was! And an aspirin when my head ached! It seems so silly now! The things just arrived, I couldn't understand it at the time . . . .'

'Well it doesn't matter,' said Judy impatiently. 'One of

the rest of us can do the wishing. Everyone has three wishes. Give the stone to Great-Gran, and she'll do it, or else I will . . . .'

'I haven't got it,' said Aunty Vi wretchedly. 'I had no idea the treasure had anything to do with that stone! I just thought I must have overlooked the things I needed. And I wanted to keep it safely somewhere till I went home. I brought it along here, but it seemed such a long way I didn't like to leave it behind, so I took it back with me to the hut, and put it on a shelf, behind the squash racquet.'

'So that's where it is now,' said Judy flatly.

'Well, well, how very unfortunate,' said Mrs Daisy Bucket.

Their dismay was interrupted by flying footsteps in the corridor, as Paddy burst into the cave, breathless with speed, and gasped out: 'They have looked all over the

island—and now they have made up their minds there is no treasure—so they are going to set fire to everything—the hut, the trees, the whole place—and then they'll sail away and never come back again!'

21
The Burnt-Out Island

'I think I got away without their seeing me, ' Paddy said, 'but I'm not too sure! I think I heard one of them give a yell, but nobody chased me. We've got to get home while we can. Give me the Pebble and I'll do it. If the island is going up in smoke there isn't any point in staying here. Please, Aunty Vi!'

'She hasn't got it,' Judy said accusingly. 'She put it in the hut.'

'In the *hut*!' cried Paddy, aghast. 'And I've only just come from the hut! I'm going right back! Whereabouts in the hut, Aunty Vi?'

'I know where and I'm coming with you!' Judy said. 'Come on, we must hurry! You lead, Paddy, and I'll be close behind you.'

She addressed the Guides and the aunts: 'Don't you make a sound till we get back again! Not a sound, do you hear? Go on Paddy! We'll simply have to run!'

They ran, but never had the corridor seemed so long and twisting. They stumbled over the falls of earth where Mrs Daisy Bucket and Judy had cascaded to join them. Overhead, the light from the setting sun shone for a moment more brightly, due to the gap in the rift, and they could only hope it was not too obvious from above.

As they ran, Paddy outlined his plan for recovering the Pebble. Too late they remembered they had only two wishes left between them. Paddy had only one single wish to rescue them with and to get them all home. If he failed, then it all fell on Judy, and first she had to get the Pebble into her own hand, and to make the right wish without a single mistake in the wording of it.

They planned the wish as they ran: Paddy flung it back over his shoulder to Judy.

'We'll say: "I wish we were all back home as we were before!" It's the only way, and if they are really burning the island I don't care about it any more! Repeat it *now*, Judy! And don't make any mistakes! We can't risk leaving anybody out—not one single person!'

'When we get to the crack in the cave we'll run out together,' he said a little later. 'You run towards the shore while I dive for the hut.'

At last the light filtering in from above changed in colour to a faint pinkish grey. A distinct smell of smoke began to waft down on them.

By the time they reached the cave and tore away the bags and boxes the air was almost too hot to breathe, and smelled horribly of burning food.

Flames burst into Paddy's face when he put a foot through the crack in the rock. The whole of the shore was alight, and flames were belching in and out of the windows and doors of the hut between the trees, while down on the shore the pirates were climbing into their boats and rowing back to their ship.

Driven back into the passage Paddy and Judy crouched out of reach of the fire, shielding their eyes from the heat, and staring between bursts of flame at the retreating crew, now pulling their boats aboard and hoisting the sails.

As they gazed after it, the great ship left the island, but was quickly lost in the wall of smoke and fire spreading across the shore. It hung like a fiery curtain over the sea, hiding the vessel from view.

There was not the slightest hope of reaching the hut while the island burned. The whole place was an inferno. Seizing a few scorched bags of food Paddy and Judy made their sober way back along the corridor to the waiting

company in the cavern, where joyful greetings turned to deep disappointment as they learned the truth.

Nobody would speak to Aunty Vi except Aunty Jay, and she just hissed two words, very spitefully: 'Toilet paper!' she sneered.

'That's quite enough,' said Mrs Daisy Bucket.

They had no water, and only a few lukewarm bottles of ginger beer. The aunts made themselves busy with rationing.

Everything tasted burnt. The guides had been frightened, but were now making the best of it. They were also very relieved at being able to talk out loud, and to sing and play games as they had done before the arrival of the pirates.

It was going to be a most uncomfortable night with everyone half sitting up against the walls of the cavern, and it became worse as the temperature rose and the cave became hotter and hotter.

Out in the passage the light that filtered down became first pink and then scarlet, and the crackle and roar of the flames in the forest trees were a very real threat to their safety.

Paddy decided to take the party lower still, and between them they managed to shift the slab that disclosed the steps into the inmost cavern.

One after another climbed down into its cooler depths, thankful for a relief from the hot cave.

The Guides snuggled down in the dark and slept. The aunts snored a little, rather wistfully. Paddy kept watch on the top step. Judy slept in fits and starts. Mrs Daisy Bucket sat up all night.

In the morning it was stuffy beyond endurance in the cavern, but the fire had moved away. It was cool enough to climb the stairs, and the slab gave no trouble.

All that day and night they stayed in the upper cavern, for the way out was deep in hot ash, and all the provisions had been burnt to a cinder.

The Guides were very brave. They knew that the hut was burnt down and that they themselves were lucky to be alive.

Mrs Daisy Bucket's stories kept them amused and they all remained quite cheerful. The next night it rained.

22
Finding the Pebble

Paddy fretted terribly. When at last he stepped out of the cave on to the shore that had been so wide and beautiful he saw it had now become a place that he could never love again.

The trees were reduced to black stumps or blackened ghosts. All the berries were gone. The streams ran black and sluggish. The hut was a mere shell, its timbers strewn across the squash court.

Deep in the warm, damp ash he waded for hours on end looking for the Pebble, though he knew almost at once that there was little hope of its ever being found.

And without it—what?

Who would tell Mr Jonathan Pickering that his island had been burned to shreds, that his treasure was lost, and that not merely two, but twenty-three or four people were living some kind of life on the burnt-out slopes of what had been his personal kingdom, with hardly any food, and nowhere to sleep at night?

But the Guides refused to be discouraged by what they saw. They fished, they put up their tents, they hollowed themselves new beds in the warm sands. They took infinite care of Mrs Daisy Bucket and were kind and polite to the aunts. They seemed in some touching and incomprehensible fashion to be pinning their faith on Paddy, relying on him to find a way out of this most unusual difficulty, and to get them home.

Judy seemed to have lost her bounce and her bossiness. She sat around looking thoughtful and depressed.

Paddy's great-grandmother reverted to her habit of earlier days, and trotted about the charred sands in her pink bloomers looking busy.

The pirates did not come back. Paddy guessed they were deeply ashamed of having burnt up the island with their prisoners on it, and did not want to go back. Judy was no longer a companion to him. Most of the time he wandered by himself, and a loneliness came over him that was lonelier than he had ever felt before.

This wasn't the island he had bought and planned for. Things had gone wrong from the beginning, and he could not see them ever coming right again. He longed above all else to get back to work, to have his school books about him, and the challenge of exams ahead, and to end this idleness that hung about him like lead.

On the next night, when there was only a slip of a moon, he stumbled across to the hut, planning to sleep in the ruins if he could find a corner that was comfortable enough.

The roof was gone. Two walls were open to the sky, and the door lay flat on its back.

Gleaming in the darkness in the middle of what had once been the squash court, lay the Pebble.

Paddy picked up the Pebble with fingers that were actually trembling. He held it in the palm of his hand, speechless with awe.

'Well?' said the Pebble politely.

'I thought you were lost for ever!' Paddy whispered. 'It has been so terrible, Pebble, I can't begin to tell you!' He placed it reverently on a rock, walking round and round it.

'It certainly was,' the Pebble agreed. 'The heat, Paddy! The dreadful heat! Fortunately, when the walls of the house fell in I was catapulted into space, and I came down in the squash court where you found me. I heard you all searching, but I couldn't do much about it. I did call out, but none of you came near enough to hear me. I was resigned to hoping a boat would come along and take you all away and I would be left in peace. You had enough to eat, I trust?'

'The Guides have been fishing,' Paddy said, 'but all the berries have been frizzled up. The food Great-Gran sent me was burnt in the cave. We've been drinking stream water, but it is still warm. Great-Gran and the aunts are just dying for a cup of tea. They'll probably wish for it once they get you back in their hands!'

'Don't risk that,' said the Pebble. 'How many wishes have you got left of your own?'

'One,' said Paddy. 'I was saving it to get myself home, and Judy has just one left too. But I'm afraid someone will do or say something silly, and something absolutely stupid will happen again.'

'Well, what would *your* wish be?' asked the Pebble.

Paddy gazed across the burnt-out shore into the distance.

'I'd like the island to be as it was before, but no Guides, no aunts, not even Great-Grandma Daisy Bucket, or Judy. It was *nice* in the old days,' he said regretfully. 'And I'd like my school books here and some lessons. And some decent food, of course. But what do you think happens when my year is up? Shall I just find myself at home, or what?'

'I should think it is unlikely that you will get yourself home without a wish,' said the Pebble. 'You may just have to put up with the island as it is now.'

'Oh I *can't*!' Paddy protested. 'I only want it as it was before, and I loved it.'

'Well, can't you wish that?' the Pebble suggested. 'If you wished the island was just as it was, say a year ago, wouldn't that get you out of all your difficulties? No Guides, no aunts, no Judy, no Great-Grandmother—and lots and lots of berries and fish. How do you like that idea?'

'Well—yes I do,' said Paddy slowly, 'but it's just about getting home in the end . . . .'

'You'll have to catch a ship,' the Pebble said. 'There was one before, wasn't there? So why shouldn't there be one again? No, don't pick me up yet! Say your wish over and over again and then go and put me back in the deep cavern and say the wish before you shut me in.'

Paddy repeated the wish two or three times before taking the Pebble in his hand and running for the cave entrance.

But before he could slip through the crack another shadow flitted after him, and caught him by the elbow. It was Judy.

'Where are you going?' she asked him urgently.

'Down the corridor,' he said shortly.

'Oh wait! Please wait!' begged Judy. 'It is such a long way to go by yourself. Do let me come too!'

'You can if you want to,' Paddy relented. It came to him suddenly that it would be good to have her company for the very last time. She had become the old Judy again, and quite soon he wouldn't be seeing her any more.

'Oh good, good!' she cried, and suddenly her arms were round his neck and she had given him a smacking kiss on the cheek. 'And you'll tell me—you *will* tell me, won't you, Paddy dear, why you are going, won't you?'

'I do wish you'd stop asking questions,' he said quite pleasantly, as they stepped through the crack in the rock, and suddenly he realised that here and now he had wished his last wish and Judy would *have* to come too.

23
Paddy and Judy

Judy did not ask any more questions, and this proved to Paddy that his last blundering wish had in fact been granted.

Overcome by the most frightful remorse he felt for her hand in the dark, and dragged her down the corridor, pouring out the whole story of the finding of the Pebble, and the vital importance of saying the words of the wish exactly as Paddy had worded it.

'I know it will be the very end, if I do,' she said sadly. 'You will still be here, and I'll be at home with the aunts and the Girl Guides and Mrs Daisy Bucket. I'd like to wish that we all go home together. It would be much easier.'

'And leave the island like it is now?' asked Paddy, aghast.

'Yes, well, I don't see why not,' said Judy. 'People hardly ever come to it, do they?'

'It looks so awful,' said Paddy. 'I can't give it back to Mr Pickering looking like a slag heap. He'd kill me! And I haven't even paid him for it yet!'

'Well then I'll wish it was all like when I came,' Judy coaxed. 'We had a lovely time, didn't we? It couldn't be better than that!'

'My great-gran would still be a hostage in the pirates' hold,' he objected. 'That doesn't seem fair, somehow.'

'She didn't seem to mind it,' Judy said stubbornly.

'What? Being seasick, and all that awful tapioca?' Paddy scoffed. 'Don't be silly!'

'We didn't know she was there being miserable,' said Judy, 'so perhaps we wouldn't know it again.'

Paddy knew he had to remain on good terms with Judy or she might wish anything she pleased, and he would be sure to come out worst. He had not one single wish of his own to escape with, and even now the news must be buzzing round the island: 'Jonathan Pickering's treasure was a wishing-stone! Everyone has three wishes! They can wish for whatever they like! We have only to find the Pebble and it's all ours!' Imagine the struggling and the scratching to hold the precious talisman, and the helplessness of himself and Judy looking on!

'Judy,' he urged, 'we simply mustn't let any of them get hold of the Pebble. You do see that, don't you?'

'Oh I do!' she agreed. 'It could be quite awful—specially if Aunty Jay got it first! We can't let that happen! But the worst bit is having only just the one wish left between us. If you hadn't been so stupid just now we could each have had one wish and put it all straight. You would have wished for the island to be lovely and beautiful again as it was when you came, and I'd have wished I could stay with you on it. Then dear Great-Gran Bucket would be safe at home, *not* with the pirates, and the aunts and the Guides would be gone. If that's what you prefer,' she sighed ruefully.

'Well we can't do it that way,' said Paddy. 'We'd have used two wishes, and we haven't got those left. And unless we hide the Pebble very securely and then wish, we may get into all kinds of new trouble. Here's the end of the passage. I'll go into the cave first. Don't you touch the Pebble whatever you do before I tell you. It doesn't make any difference now whatever I say or do! It's too late,' he added bitterly.

It seemed a long time since he had climbed down the steps into the darkest cave of all, and just for a minute he hesitated with one foot inside the hole and one out.

'Are you sure you know what to wish for?' he asked Judy. 'It is just *so* important, Judy! I'd rather we all went home together than have Great-Gran left in the pirates' hold, maybe for always. I'll give up the island—I really will, if you promise to save her as well! We'll put the Pebble back in the corner, and you can wish on it. Tell me now just what you mean to say!'

Judy hesitated on the highest step. He could see her swinging her foot in the twilight.

'Actually we are all quite safe as we are at present,' she murmured. 'It's only the island that is so dreadful. If I wish it was young and beautiful again nobody is going to get hurt, and we can still all have a lovely time together!'

'What about Jonathan Pickering's curse?' Paddy warned her. 'About not having more than two people here together? Any disaster could happen again, and some of it could be even *worse*! You and I wouldn't have any wishes left, and if the aunts get hold of the stone we don't know where they'd land us.'

'All the same, I think I'll risk it,' said Judy, coming slowly down the steps.

'If you do,' said Paddy, speaking very clearly and distinctly, 'I shall never, NEVER speak to you again as long as I live!'

Judy passed him without speaking.

'Do you hear me?' Paddy repeated, even more clearly and distinctly. 'If you wish that wish I promise and declare that for the whole of the rest of my life I will never NEVER speak to you again!'

He fully expected Judy to say: 'That's all right by me!' or some such dismissive phrase, but she said nothing at all.

At last, in a small subdued voice she said: 'All right, Paddy, I won't! I won't make that wish! But I'll have to get us all home together, you know, or otherwise I won't see you for months and months and months and I couldn't bear that. I know you want to stay here, but we don't know how or when you are going to come home, and I really don't see how I can wish so you stay here without us. I don't believe you really want to anyway!'

'Yes I do,' said Paddy stoutly. He found that in fact he did.

'Well, what do you want me to say, then?'

'Just say, "I wish the island was the same as it was—what? Six months, eight months, nine months ago?"' said Paddy. 'That covers everything. My great-gran was still at home, but I don't know about you and me. I've lost all count of time. I know the Girl Guides haven't been here all that long, neither have the aunts, though it seems like a lifetime. But you and I and Great-Gran Bucket might have been here for ever, and me even longer than that.'

'Then we'd better not wish too far back,' said Judy nervously.

She watched Paddy replace the Pebble in a very dark corner.

'Come on!' he said bravely. 'Goodbye, Pebble!'

The Pebble could not even answer him now.

'And lots of thanks,' he added.

He surprised himself that he did not feel more pain in knowing that this was the very end. It *did* matter, of course, but there was no other way out, and what must be, must be.

In spite of the deep darkness he closed his eyes, and heard Judy reciting steadily: 'I wish the island was just exactly as it was eight months ago!'

Nothing happened.

Only, when he opened his eyes he could not see the faint outline of Judy beside him, and he could not see her hand on the Pebble.

'Try again,' he told her. 'Pick it up and hold it in your hand.'

But Judy was not here. He fumbled round the cavern trying to find her, but met only rocks and stones and the hard base of the stone staircase.

He climbed the steps, thinking she had gone on ahead of him, into the upper cave and the corridor, but when he reached the top step he bumped his head on the stone slab that shut away the deep cavern from the rest.

He moved from side to side, but met nothing but strong resistance. Paddy knew blind fear as he pushed and heaved and battered at the rock. It was as solid as eternity.

Nothing he could do, *nothing* gave him a glimmer of hope that he would ever get out again.

He flopped rather than fell, to the bottom of the flight, and lay on the ground exhaused. When he roused himself the eye of the Pebble was shining in the dark, and towards this he crept on his knees, beseeching: 'Oh Pebble! Please, please help me to get out! Please, please do!'

The Pebble did not speak, but something urged Paddy to try again. He struggled up the steps, and this time the slab slid gently away as his head touched it, and he scrambled out nearly crying with relief.

'Thank you, Pebble! Oh thank you!' he called back into the darkness of the deep cave, before pushing the rock into place, and covering it safely with the three stones.

He started at a jogtrot down the passage, and fresh, sweet island air sifted down to him through the crack above his head, full of the scents he thought had gone for ever. He looked for the tumble of earth and stones that had been his great-grandmother's entry, and again for Judy's landslide, but both had disappeared. The passage went on and on, winding, turning, twisting, always with the same haunting fragrance he remembered from the days of his first arrival. He could even hear the birds singing overhead, and presently the faint, far lapping of the sea.

The light grew brighter, and he slipped through the crack into the cave on the shore, bare of provisions now, but opening on to the sparkling white sands of the little bay where he had fished and turned cartwheels, and, truth to tell, longed for a little company.

There was no company now. No Guides, no aunts, no great-grandmother, no Judy, but neither was there any trace of fire.

The hut was standing just where it used to stand. The squash court invited a game. The bushes round the hut were heavy with berries.

Paddy wandered into the house to inspect every corner. He found his bed and his squash racquet, and lying close by, his fishing rod.

The quiet was enormous. Just the birds and the waves and the pad-pad of his own footsteps on the sand. Not even a little breeze to stir the great sails of the palm tree branches.

'I didn't know it would be quite like this,' Paddy thought, and some of the joy seeped out of his heart.

'I might as well catch a fish for my dinner,' he said, picking up his fishing rod and bait tin. But first he would have to catch some tiddlers for bait.

Striding down the beach as purposefully as he could, he came face to face with somebody coming round the corner of the rocks.

It was Mr Jonathan Pickering.

24
Going Home

'Good afternoon!' said Jonathan Pickering.

Paddy could not find a word to say. At last he stammered: 'Have you come about the rent?'

'More or less,' said his landlord, 'but I just wanted to know how you were doing here on your own. Enjoying yourself?'

'I don't know,' Paddy said lamely. 'Sort of yes, sort of no. Mostly yes, I think! But a lot of no too. Do you know how long I have been here, please, Mr Pickering?'

'About eight months,' Jonathan Pickering told him. 'Quite a long time for a young one to be on his tod! You have looked after my treasure, I trust!'

Paddy said he had.

'And I've run out of wishes,' he said regretfully.

'Ah! The dear old Pebble!' Jonathan Pickering said. 'Well, I hope you have had your money's worth! Quite a brave chap, you are, to stay here all these weeks by yourself. You have grown out of your trousers, I see! That is what worried your great-grandmother, Mrs Daisy Bucket. "The boy will have no clothes left to wear!" she told me this morning when she came into the office. I've got some new jeans for you in my boat.'

Paddy stiffened a very little.

'I don't need smart clothes here,' he protested. 'And about the rent, I'm afraid I haven't brought any money with me.'

Jonathan Pickering looked at him indulgently.

'Not to worry,' he said kindly. 'We'll settle all that up at the end of the year, when we get back to my office. Your great-grandmother just asked me to tell you that your parents are due back from America on Saturday, and what is she to say to them?'

'She *knows* . . . ?' Paddy asked.

'Of course she knows. She is a very intelligent old lady!' said Jonathan Pickering.

'Did she tell you about everything?' Paddy pursued.

'She said you would tell me,' said Jonathan. 'Oh and by the way, she sent you a peppermint!'

They sat together in the shade of a palm tree, sucking peppermints. Paddy related the events of his island life, not in detail, since one happening ran into another and tripped each other up, but in general, wondering, even as he talked, how the eight months had frittered away, and how he could

find himself here and now exactly as he had been all that time ago, and yet nothing to show for it.

'You think it has all been worth while?' Jonathan Pickering asked at the end.

'Yes—well yes, I do. I think I do.'

'And you want to go on to the end of the lease, is that it?'

'Yes. I think so. I think I do!'

'In that case,' Mr Jonathan Pickering said, 'I had better go back to my motor boat. I'll throw your jeans ashore. Your great-grandmother also sent you a case of food. I'll tell her she'll have to make up some likely tale to tell your parents, won't she?'

'What about the aunts, and Judy and the Girl Guides?' Paddy wanted to know. It seemed unlikely that so many people would be able to keep quiet about so great a secret.

'Oh they don't remember a thing about it,' Jonathan Pickering chuckled. 'Judy just might. There's another intelligent woman for you! But you don't need to worry about *her*!'

'Just one thing,' Paddy urged. 'You left the island, didn't you? Why did you go away?'

'Ah!' said Jonathan Pickering wisely. 'That's another story! What's good for a holiday island isn't always good for life, not when you are a man. There's not enough to do. How much have you done since you came here?'

'Pretty well nothing,' Paddy admitted.

'Ha!' said Jonathan Pickering. 'Then you'll be all behind the rest of them when you get back to school. Well done!'

'I shan't!' said Paddy hotly. 'And if I had my books here I would have been way ahead of them as usual!'

'Ha!' said Jonathan Pickering again. 'Well, isn't that just too bad? Goodbye, old boy! I'm glad you like my island and haven't lost out by staying here! Well done, and all that! I'll come back for you in four months' time. Cheerio!'

He got up and strode across the sand in the direction of the far rocks.

Pride kept Paddy glued to his place, but when he saw Mr Pickering's head growing smaller and smaller beyond the point he leapt up and began to run at top speed to catch him up.

The roar of the motor drowned his shout as he called across the bay: 'Mr Pickering! Please stop! Please wait for me, sir! Please take me too!'

Jonathan Pickering put his engine into reverse and drove the boat into the channel where he had already landed Paddy's folded jeans and the large box of food.

'Come on then!' he said.

Paddy leapt for the boat. He hit his shin on the side and for a moment the pain was too excruciating for him to remember what was all-important to his return.

Finally he gasped out the words: 'Oh please, Mr Pickering, can we go back just for a minute? No more than that! I promise I won't keep you any longer! But I've left my dad's squash racquet on the shelf in the house, and I promised—I *promised* I would bring it back to him!'

While he was fetching the racquet Jonathan Pickering unpacked Mrs Daisy Bucket's hamper, and set out their dinner on the prow.

On the following pages you will find some other exciting Beaver Books to look out for in your local bookshop